"Yes, I'm Abigail Connors."

"I'm Marcus Wellington of Wellington Agency. Your father—"

"Yes, I'm aware that my father hired you to watch over me. I tried to tell him that your services weren't needed, but he insisted."

"He just wants to make sure you are safe while you are here."

"Yes, well, I'm sure I will be."

Marcus chuckled. "I know you will be as long as I'm responsible for seeing that you are."

How dare he laugh at her! "You are quite confident of yourself, aren't you, Mr. Wellington?"

He irritated her even further by grinning at her. A dimple appeared near his mouth. But his tone was serious when he answered, "My business depends on me being able to do what I say I will, Miss Connors. And I've promised your father that you will be safe while under my agency's watchfulness."

JANET LEE BARTON and her husband, Dan, have recently moved to Oklahoma and feel blessed to have at least one daughter and her family living nearby. Janet loves being able to share her faith and love of the Lord through her writing. She's very happy that the kind of romances the Lord has called her to write can be read by and shared with women of all ages.

Books by Janet Lee Barton

HEARTSONG PRESENTS
HP434—Family Circle
HP532—A Promise Made
HP562—Family Ties
HP623—A Place Called Home
HP644—Making Amends
HP689—Unforgettable
HP710—To Love Again
HP730—With Open Arms
HP745—Family Reunion
HP759—Stirring Up Romance
HP836—A Love for Keeps

A Love
All Her Own

Janet Lee Barton

Heartsong Presents

To my Lord and Savior for showing me the way and to my family for their love and support always.

A note from the Author:
I love to hear from my readers! You may correspond with me by writing:

Janet Lee Barton
Author Relations
PO Box 721
Uhrichsville, OH 44683

ISBN 978-1-60260-439-1

A LOVE ALL HER OWN

All scripture quotations are taken from the King James Version of the Bible.

All of the characters and events in this book are fictitious. Any resemblance to actual persons, living or dead, or to actual events is purely coincidental.

Our mission is to publish and distribute inspirational products offering exceptional value and biblical encouragement to the masses.

PRINTED IN THE U.S.A.

one

Eureka Springs, Arkansas,
July 20, 1886

Abigail Connors sniffed and threw off her covers. She was through with this crying. It wasn't going to change a thing. She'd done enough of that over the past week and a half—ever since her world had collapsed around her. Much as she wanted to pretend it was all a nightmare, there was no denying it. She'd lost the man she'd loved for years and the love of the niece she adored—all in one afternoon. And she had no one to blame but herself.

Fresh tears threatened, even when she thought she couldn't possibly have any left, but she swiped at her eyes and held her weeping at bay. It wasn't going to do her any good, and she couldn't stay in bed forever. As it was, enough talk about her was probably circulating around town, now that her wedding had been called off. She pulled on her wrapper and yanked the cord to summon her parents' housekeeper.

In minutes, Laura appeared. "Miss Abigail, I'm so glad to see you up and about! Would you like some breakfast?" It was obvious that the woman had been worried about her. During those first few days when Abigail couldn't have cared less if she ever ate again, everyone in the house had practically begged her to eat. Laura had prepared all her favorites to no avail. But the woman looked so hopeful this morning that Abigail couldn't disappoint her.

"Perhaps after I've had a bath, Laura. Please prepare that for me now, and then you can make me some tea and toast."

The housekeeper set about doing as asked at once. By the time Abigail was finished bathing and was trying to decide what she needed to do next, Laura arrived with a tray laden with tea, toast, and an egg cooked just the way Abigail liked it. For the first time in days, Abigail felt hungry. "Thank you, Laura. I think I'll be going home today, so if you would just see that my things get home, I would appreciate it."

Laura didn't say anything, but Abigail had a feeling the housekeeper didn't approve and would go running to her mother with the news. Nevertheless, it was time. She had to make plans. She could not stay in Eureka Springs and watch Nate Brooks start a new life with Meagan Snow. She couldn't stay and see the disgust in her niece Natalie's eyes when the little girl looked at her. Nor could she stay and be laughed at behind her back. She could not, would not do it. Going anywhere would be better.

Abigail ate her breakfast and was on her second cup of tea when her mother's light knock sounded on the door. "Come in, Mama."

"Abigail, dear, what's this Laura tells me about you going home?" her mother asked, gracefully sweeping into the room. She looked lovely as always, dressed in a green-and-white-striped morning dress, with not a hair out of place. "I'm not sure you are ready to—"

"It's time, Mama. I can't stay with you and Papa forever, and I can't stay in Eureka Springs, either. Not with the. . ." She couldn't finish the sentence. She didn't even want to think about Nate's upcoming marriage to Meagan Snow.

"But dear, you don't want to make a hasty decision. Give yourself time—"

"Mama, please. I just can't stay here. Don't you see?" Her parents had been so very kind and patient with her the last few days, even after she'd admitted what an awful person she was. They had assured her of their love and insisted she stay with them until she felt she could cope with her heartache, but she knew she'd disappointed them. Abigail felt she had to get away, but she wasn't quite sure where to go. "Mama, I must get out of Eureka Springs."

"Why don't you get dressed and then come down to your papa's study? We can talk to him about it. He'll know what to do."

"Mama, he's not going to want me going anywhere. I—"

"Abigail, dear, your father and I have your best interests at heart. You know that. We will hear you out, and then together, we'll all decide what is best."

Abigail sighed. There was no way around it. She was going to have to discuss this with her father. She needed a plan, and she needed it quickly.

❧

Abigail dressed in a pale blue morning dress, and Laura dressed her hair for her, arranging it on top of her head as was in fashion. Before leaving the room, Abigail pinched her cheeks to give them a little color, knowing her papa would try to find a reason to keep her under his care a little longer. Taking a deep breath, she opened the bedroom door and went down to his study.

Her father was sitting at his desk, writing, while her mother was looking out the front window, a cup of tea in her hand. "I just don't know, Jacob," her mother said but cut her sentence off when she noticed Abigail enter the room.

"Don't know what, Mama?" Abigail mustered a smile. "What to do with me?"

Her father rewarded her with a chuckle. "That would probably sum it up nicely, dear. You have presented us a challenge from time to time."

Abigail went over and kissed the top of her father's head. "Yes, I know. Mama has been telling you that I think it's time to leave, hasn't she?"

"She has. I don't think it is a good idea."

"Somehow that doesn't surprise me, Papa. But I must find a way to. . .get on with my life." Abigail heard the wobble in her voice and hoped her parents didn't notice it.

Her mother poured a cup of tea and handed it to her. "Here dear. We'll figure out something."

"Thank you, Mama." Abigail took a sip and continued. "I'd like to get away for a while."

"Away? You aren't just talking about going back to your house, are you?"

"No, Papa. I—I want to get out of Eureka Springs for a while." *Maybe for the rest of my life,* Abigail thought. But she didn't voice the wish.

"Georgette dear, I'd like a cup of that tea, please." Abigail's father waited until he'd taken a sip from the cup her mother handed him. "Where are you thinking you'd like to go?"

She took a deep breath. "Europe."

Her father almost choked on the warm liquid he'd swallowed. "Europe!" He stood up and began to pace the room. "Abigail, Europe is much too far away. What if something happened and you needed us?"

"Papa, I'm sure I'd be all right." But the thought did give her pause. Much as she thought of herself as independent, Abigail had never really been away from home without her parents.

He shook his head. "No. I don't think that's a good idea at all. Please dear, just give things time."

"Oh Papa, I don't think I can stand staying in the same town where everyone knows me—and knows that my engagement has been broken *and* that Nate will be marrying Meagan Snow very soon. Everyone I know will be laughing and talking behind my back." Abigail could feel the tears and knew she couldn't hold them at bay much longer. "I can't stay knowing that my Natalie doesn't want anything to do with me—" Her voice broke on a sob. "I just can't do that. I need a change. I have to get away, Papa. I just have to."

Jacob Connors gathered her in his arms and rocked her back and forth. "Oh, my Abby. Just let me think on it a little while. I believe I can come up with something closer than half a continent and an ocean away. Don't go home just yet. Have dinner with us, and I'll try to have an answer for you by then."

Abigail sighed in relief. Her father was going to help her. She was going to be able to get away from all the hurt and humiliation. "Thank you, Papa," she whispered.

❧

Marcus Wellington stopped by Western Union as he did first thing every morning, noon, and afternoon. In his business, he was liable to get several telegrams a day. The telegrapher handed him two new ones.

"This one from Mr. Connors in Eureka Springs just came in a few minutes ago, Marcus," Harold Dillard said.

"Thank you, Harold." Marcus took the telegrams and moved over to the end of the counter to read them. He tore into Mr. Connors's first. He hadn't heard from the man in several months, but whatever he needed, Marcus would get to first. He read:

Marcus, need your help. Daughter is coming to Hot Springs soon. Need you to have protection for her. Can you take care of it for me?

Marcus waited until the customer Harold was helping left. "I need to reply to this one right away, Harold."

The clerk gave him a pad and pencil, and Marcus wrote: *Jacob. Will be glad to. Let me know the details. Marcus.* He handed it to Harold. "This needs to go out right away."

"I can do that, Marcus." Harold read it over and began transmitting.

"I'll wait a few minutes—just to make sure he's not on the other end waiting for my reply—to send another," Marcus said, walking over to look out the window. He couldn't help but wonder why Jacob's daughter would be coming to Hot Springs by herself, but it didn't matter. The man had asked him a favor, and there was no way he'd turn him down. If it hadn't been for Jacob Connors, the Wellington Agency wouldn't exist. Marcus had just about exhausted his resources two years ago when he'd finally approached his father's good friend and banker, Jacob Connors. He wasn't sure if that was the only reason the man had lent him the money to start his detective/protective agency, but they both had reason to be glad he did. Many people had thought that his business would fail within a month or two, but they'd been wrong. The Wellington Agency would never compete with the Pinkerton Agency, and that was fine with Marcus. He had no desire to be that big. Still, his business was doing so well he was making plans to open offices all across the state, and he owed it all to Jacob Connors.

The telegraph machine started working, alerting Marcus that a message was coming in. Harold was writing out the code. "You were right. He must have been waiting for you." Harold handed Marcus the paper:

Thank you. Will be sending details in the next day or so.

Marcus sent a reply saying, *Message received. Will be looking for next one.* There was nothing else to do until he knew when Jacob's daughter would be arriving. He'd check his schedule and think about whom he could trust to watch over Miss Connors. He folded the message and headed for the door. "See you later, Harold."

&

When Abigail joined her parents for dinner, she couldn't tell if her father had come up with a plan or not, but she knew he would let her know in his own way and his own time. She just hoped it would be before she lost what appetite she had for the meal she knew Laura had prepared with her tastes in mind. It was the first time since she'd been staying with her parents that she had joined them for dinner, and the housekeeper had made her favorites, from baked ham to scalloped potatoes and rolls.

Her father seated her mother and took his place at the head of the table. Then he looked at Abigail. "I think I have a plan. But let's ask a blessing for our food first, and then I'll tell you all about it."

Abigail bowed her head while her father gave the blessing.

"Dear Lord, we thank You for this day. We thank You that our Abby is joining us for dinner tonight. Father, we ask that the plans we draw up for her are in Your will. And we ask You to bless this food we are about to eat. In Jesus' name. Amen."

As her mother began to dish up the meal, her father laid out the plan he'd come up with.

"For some time now, I've been thinking about investing in a bathhouse in Hot Springs. I believe the town could support another one, but I want it to be very nice."

"But Jacob, what does that have to do with Abigail?" his wife asked, handing him his plate.

"Well, I don't know who I'd trust more to investigate the

bathhouses already in business than my daughter. Abigail wants to get away. I don't think it really matters where, does it, daughter?"

Abigail shrugged. "Not particularly. I've heard that Hot Springs is a very nice place to visit. I'm not sure it's far enough away, though. Some of my friends are the ones who told me about it."

"Dear, I know you wish to get away." Her mother handed Abigail a filled plate. "But I would rest so much better if I knew you were in the state. I would worry so if you were to travel abroad."

"Well, I suppose I could check out the bathhouses for Papa. If I hate it there, I'm sure I can go somewhere else."

"I think you'll like it fine," her father said. "There is even more to do there than in Eureka Springs. And we have friends who you could go to if you needed anything. Your mother and I have known the Wellingtons for a long time. They will show you around and help you get acquainted quickly."

Abigail wanted to protest, but deep down, she had to admit that she'd feel more comfortable if she knew some people in the area whom she could turn to if needed. It appeared that her parents understood her need to get out of town. That alone had her appetite coming back, and Abigail found she was actually very hungry.

"That will be nice. The Wellingtons. I'll look for them," Abigail said before taking a bite of ham.

"You won't have to. Their son will be meeting your train," her father said. "He owns the Wellington Agency. It's a detective/protective agency, and I've asked him to watch over you while you are there."

Abigail almost choked on the ham she'd just swallowed. "Papa, I don't need someone to watch every move I make!"

"Abigail, dear. You are my daughter, and you stand to have a sizable inheritance one day. I don't want anything happening to you," her father said quietly.

"But—"

"Abigail, Marcus Wellington is going to make sure you are safe. That is all. More than likely, you won't even know who it is he has watching you at any given time. His agency is growing and getting good reports from all over the country. Your mother and I know his family, and I know him to be an honorable man."

"But, Papa—"

"Abigail. It really isn't going to matter whether you are here in the States or in Europe. Be assured I will hire someone to watch over you no matter where you go. And you are going to have someone to turn to if you need them—whether you like it or not."

two

The trip by train to Hot Springs was long, but Abigail was so relieved to get out of Eureka Springs she hardly noticed. It had taken longer than she expected—or wanted—to pack and close her home for an extended stay away, but finally she had left on the evening train on Thursday, August 5. From Eureka Springs, she'd gone through Fayetteville and on to Fort Smith. Arriving there late that night, she switched from the Frisco line to the Iron Mountain line, where her father had booked a sleeping berth for her. She'd thought she wouldn't be able to sleep, but the rocking motion of the train lulled her into a deep slumber so that she woke refreshed and excited to finish the last leg of the trip. After freshening up and eating breakfast at Malvern, she switched trains for the last time and watched the scenery pass by, glad that she would be at Hot Springs that afternoon.

Abigail had been very busy ever since she agreed to go to Hot Springs instead of Europe. The relief she felt that she wouldn't have to stay in Eureka Springs and be humiliated further by the gossip and speculation as to why Nate was going to marry Meagan Snow instead of her was huge. It energized her enough to decide what to take with her and arrange to have her home closed until she returned—if she ever did. At the moment, she couldn't imagine wanting to go back to Eureka Springs, but she wasn't about to voice that opinion to her parents.

As the train neared Hot Springs, Abigail looked out the

window and could see the edge of the Ouachita Mountains getting closer. She wondered if Hot Springs was going to be that much different from her hometown and then decided that it didn't matter. What did was that she didn't know anyone here. There would be no one to know her background or to gossip about her.

She could feel both the excitement and apprehension of being on her own in a strange place begin to mount as the train slowed down and entered Hot Springs. The city seemed to be situated in a narrow valley between mountains, with pines scaling one mountainside while hickory, oaks, and other hardwoods covered the opposite mountainside. She caught glimpses of pink and purple flowers here and there. As the train eased to a stop and blew its whistle at the train depot, Abigail stood and shook out her skirts. She was glad she'd chosen a frock of brown and beige foulard. It didn't show the dust and ash from train travel quite as badly as other colors.

Her papa had told her that there would be someone to meet her at the train depot, and as she gathered her parasol and reticule and made her way to the exit, she hoped he was right. Suddenly, the fact that she was alone in a strange place weighed down on her, and she realized that she wasn't quite as brave and independent as she wanted everyone to think. She stepped off the train and looked around, only she wasn't sure whom she was looking for or what he might look like.

⁂

Over the last two weeks, Marcus had received a detailed letter and several telegrams from Jacob Connors. He'd found out that Miss Connors had been planning on getting married recently but that the marriage had been called off and she wanted to get away. She'd be checking out some business dealings for her father while she was there. The man didn't expect her to be watched around the clock—he just wanted her safe. Although Jacob didn't give Marcus any more information than that, they'd kept the telegraph lines busy while they came up with an elaborate plan to make sure Abigail Connors got to Hot Springs safely—and hopefully without her suspecting anything, at least while she was traveling. Jacob had told Marcus that Abigail knew someone from the Wellington Agency would be watching over her—whether she liked it or not—once she got to Hot Springs, but she wasn't to know that she'd be watched all the way to Hot Springs.

From what Jacob had told him, Marcus had a feeling Miss Connors was quite independent and, if he wasn't mistaken, quite a bit spoiled. Still, she was Jacob's daughter, and he was going to do all he could to keep her safe and out of trouble during her stay in Hot Springs.

With most of his agents on assignment or on much-needed leave, Marcus had assigned Luke Monroe, a young man whom he'd been able to clear of a crime he didn't commit but had served time in prison for, to see that Miss Connors reached Hot Springs safely.

At twenty, Luke had no living relatives and no place to call home. Marcus had found he just couldn't let the young man fend for himself. Although his name had been cleared, Luke would have a hard time finding a job, and Marcus had wanted to help.

When he'd asked Luke if he wanted to join the Wellington Agency and learn the business from desk clerk up, Luke hadn't hesitated a moment. "Oh, yes, sir! I'd love to help somebody one day the way you helped me," he'd said.

That was all it took. Marcus owned the building that housed his office and his own apartment, and he happened to have a vacancy *and* a need for a building manager. He offered the apartment as part of Luke's pay, along with a salary. In the meantime, he'd train the young man to be a good agent.

When he offered Luke the position, he'd thought he'd seen the sheen of tears in the young man's eyes. "Sir," Luke had said, "I'll never make you sorry for helping me. I promise you. I want to be one of the best agents you have, and I'll work hard to become just that."

"I can't ask for more than that, Luke. You can move in the apartment today—it's furnished. And you can start work tomorrow."

That had been six months ago, and although this was Luke's first real assignment, Marcus didn't have one doubt that Luke would do all he could to do the job right, to see that Abigail Connors got on the right trains and that she was not bothered by anyone on her way, all without her knowing she was being watched.

Marcus had sent Luke to Eureka Springs two days before Abigail was to leave. Jacob had met him, and they'd arranged for him to be at the train station when Jacob and his wife took Abigail to catch her train so that he would know exactly who it was he'd been hired to keep safe.

Afterward, Jacob had sent Marcus a telegram letting him know that Abigail and the agent were on their way. All Marcus had to do was meet her train when it came in that afternoon.

Normally, Luke did a lot of the mail and telegram sorting from the desk across the room. Then he'd give it to Marcus in order of importance. Marcus had gotten used to the young man sharing the office with him but knew that since he'd put him in the field, the young man would be wanting another outside assignment soon. Marcus read the other telegrams he'd received that morning and decided what needed to be answered right away, keeping an eye on the clock so that he wouldn't be late to meet the train. When his telephone rang one quick and two sharp rings, he jumped and hurried over to the wall where it was installed. He still wasn't used to the modern convenience, but his parents had convinced him that if he was planning to expand his business, he really should have one put in at his office. It stood silent most of the time, and when it did ring, most times it was his mother—making sure it worked.

Marcus wasn't the least bit surprised to hear her voice on the line now. "Marcus dear, what time is it that Jacob and Georgette's daughter arrives today?"

"She's coming in on the afternoon train, Mother."

"Are you sure you don't want to bring her by this afternoon, dear?"

"Jacob said she would most likely be tired from travel and that she would probably want to get settled into the hotel."

"I do wish he'd just have sent her here. We have plenty of room and—"

"Maybe you can convince her to stay with you and Papa once she gets to know you, Mother."

"Perhaps. When your father telegraphed Jacob, though, it sounded as if he thought she'd want to stay in the hotel. But we'll see what we can do to change her mind."

Marcus smiled, knowing that his mother would do just that. "I'm sure you will, Mother. I'll bring her by tomorrow as planned, all right?"

"That will be fine, son. I have a nice dinner planned. Will you be over for dinner tonight?"

"Not this evening, Mother, but thank you. I need to make sure the arrangements I've made for Miss Connors will work out."

"All right then, son. I'll see you tomorrow. I am so glad you had a telephone put in."

Marcus couldn't contain his chuckle. "Yes, I know. I am, too, Mother." He replaced the receiver and looked at the clock. He'd finish the schedules he made each week for his agents and then head down to the depot. He was anxious to meet Abigail Connors and try to figure out what he'd be requiring the agents he assigned to her to do. He prayed that she wouldn't be too much of a handful, but in reading between the lines of Jacob's correspondence, Marcus had a feeling she would be.

❧

Abigail stood at the bottom of the steps for only a minute or two before a man whose size alone was slightly intimidating approached her. He was broad shouldered and dressed impeccably. . .and he towered over her. He took his hat off and addressed her.

"Miss Connors? Abigail Connors?" He looked down at her with a smile that brought out a dimple in his cheek and made her catch her breath.

He must be the man her father had arranged to meet her, Abigail thought. She found herself looking into the bluest eyes she'd ever seen, and they seemed to be looking right into her soul. "Yes, I'm Abigail Connors."

"I'm Marcus Wellington of Wellington Agency. Your father—"

"Yes, I'm aware that my father hired you to watch over me. I tried to tell him that your services weren't needed, but he insisted."

"He just wants to make sure you are safe while you are here."

"Yes, well, I'm sure I will be."

Marcus chuckled. "I know you will be as long as I'm

responsible for seeing that you are."

How dare he laugh at her! "You are quite confident of yourself, aren't you, Mr. Wellington?"

He irritated her even further by grinning at her. A dimple appeared near his mouth. But his tone was serious when he answered, "My business depends on me being able to do what I say I will, Miss Connors. And I've promised your father that you will be safe while under my agency's watchfulness. Now, let's get your bags, and I'll see you to your hotel."

It appeared Mr. Wellington was as bossy as he was confident. There was no point, however, in arguing with the man. Her father had hired his agency, and she really couldn't do anything about that. Besides, he was the son of good friends of her parents, and she'd given her parents enough to go through lately. She would put up with him if she had to, but she didn't like his cockiness one bit—even if he did try to cover it with the most beautiful smile she'd ever seen.

Marcus led her into the train depot, where they waited for her baggage to be unloaded from the train. Once it was brought over and he saw the trunk and bags she said were hers, Marcus arranged for the luggage to be sent over to the Arlington Hotel, where she would be staying. Then he hired a hackney to take them to the hotel. That he knew how to take charge couldn't be disputed—he seemed to command respect without demanding it.

He helped her into the cab and then took a seat beside her. "I do hope you enjoy your visit to our city, Miss Connors. Your father said you would be taking care of some business for him while you are here."

Dear Papa. "Yes. He's thinking of investing in a bathhouse venture and wants me to look into the ones here in Hot Springs."

"The hotel where you are staying is on what we call Bathhouse Row. You'll see that there are a few new bathhouses under construction. You do have them in Eureka Springs, don't you?"

"Just a few, although our hotels are built near the springs for the guests' convenience." Abigail glanced about as they rode through downtown and noticed that Hot Springs seemed to be way ahead of her hometown in some ways. The boardwalks that were only talked about in Eureka Springs were a reality here and were uniformly wide. Her mother would love them. She'd be sure and write her parents about it. Perhaps they could nudge the city leaders to move a little faster.

Mr. Wellington pointed to the buildings they were passing by. "Here are the bathhouses. There is the Palace Bathhouse, and the one right next to it is the Independent. Then there is the Hale Bathhouse and the Big Iron."

As he pointed them all out, Abigail was impressed with how nice they looked standing in a row with magnolia trees lining the street that ran in front of them. The huge white blossoms of the magnolias smelled wonderful. Pine trees grew up the mountain behind them, yet on the mountain behind the buildings across the street, there seemed to be mostly oak and hickory trees, leafy and green. It really was a beautiful setting, and Abigail looked forward to visiting each bathhouse to see what it offered.

"Here we are," Mr. Wellington said as the hackney pulled up in front of a very nice hotel. "I think you'll enjoy your stay at the Arlington. It's one of the nicest in town. The Hays will be even nicer once they get through remodeling, but it isn't due to open until next year. For now, you are staying at one of the best hotels in town."

He paid the driver and helped her down from the cab. Abigail didn't offer to reimburse him—she supposed it would be included in what her father paid the man. He did see her into the hotel, and she was impressed by the lovely interior. The desk clerk was very nice when she registered, and a bellboy came immediately to show her to her room.

"Her bags will be sent over from the train depot. Please see that she gets them as soon as they arrive," Marcus said to the man at the desk.

"Certainly, Mr. Wellington."

Marcus Wellington followed her and the bellboy up the stairs to the second-floor rooms she'd been given. When she looked at him questioningly, he bent and whispered in her ear, "I make it a practice to check out the rooms of my clients to make sure there are no surprises."

"What do you mean?"

"Just to make sure your windows lock, the door locks properly, that kind of thing."

"Oh, all right. Thank you."

The bellboy stopped outside a door just two away from the main staircase, and Mr. Wellington waited until the boy unlocked and opened it for Abigail. They entered a small sitting room with a bedroom off to the side. While the bellboy was explaining where everything was, Marcus made sure the locks on the windows were secure. He took the key from the young man and made sure that the door did lock, and then he handed it to Abigail.

The bellboy left, promising to bring up Abigail's bags when they arrived, and Marcus stood just outside the door. "Is there anything I can get you, Miss Connors? Would you like company for dinner?"

"No, thank you. I'll eat here at the hotel and have an early evening. I'm rather tired from the travel."

"I've promised your father and my parents that I will bring you over tomorrow to meet them."

Abigail had also promised her father that she would meet the Wellingtons and check in with them from time to time, so she agreed. "What time will be best for your mother?"

"She thought you might take tea with them in the afternoon, if that appeals to you."

"Yes, that will be nice. What time?"

"I'll pick you up about three o'clock, if that is acceptable."

"That will be fine."

Marcus turned just in time to see the bellboy and another young man bringing up a trunk. "Is that for Miss Connors?"

"Yes, sir. There are several more pieces, too."

Marcus waited until the trunk and two more bags had been delivered to Abigail's room. She had to admit she was glad he was there. She wasn't used to strange men handling her things. She tipped the young men when the last bag was set down. "Thank you. Will you please ask the desk clerk to send someone up to help me unpack?"

"I'll be glad to. Thank you, ma'am," the first young man answered. They both smiled as they turned to go back downstairs.

"Everything is here?" Marcus asked her.

"Yes, I believe so. I'll let you know if I find anything missing."

He nodded. "Good. I'll see you tomorrow then. And Miss Connors. . ."

"Yes?"

"Be assured that you'll be safe here." He tipped his hat and turned to leave.

Abigail still wasn't sure how she felt about all her comings and goings being watched, but her father had insisted. "Thank you. I'm sure my father will be pleased."

"Have a good evening." Mr. Wellington tipped his hat to her and turned to go back downstairs.

Abigail closed her door and locked it. Then she crossed over to the windows that looked down on the street below. She wondered what was taking so long, but she watched until Mr. Wellington finally came out of the hotel. He was with several other men, and Abigail wondered if they would be some of the men he assigned to her. When he got to the street, he looked up toward her window, and Abigail quickly moved behind the drapes so that he wouldn't know she saw him. He pulled out his pocket watch and looked at it then turned. He did not use one of the hackneys lined up outside, taking off on foot, instead. He crossed the street and headed back in the direction of the train depot. She wondered where his offices were. And she couldn't help but wonder who he'd have watching over her. What surprised her most, however, was that although she didn't like his cockiness one bit, she couldn't deny that it made her feel better knowing he was in charge of making sure she was safe.

❧

Almost as soon as he'd met Miss Connors, Marcus had decided to make some changes in the assignments he'd given his men. Once downstairs in the lobby, he met with the agents he'd assigned to watch over Abigail Connors during her stay. His free agents had been there, reading papers when he brought her in so they could see what she looked like.

Now he handed out assignments on what days and times they'd be responsible for watching her—with one change. "Benson, I'm going to take over the responsibility of escorting her wherever she needs to go, and it has nothing to do with your capabilities. I have a feeling Miss Connors could be slightly demanding, and since she is the daughter of the man who helped me get this business started, I feel I'm the one who should deal with all that. I'll have you assigned to watch her while she's here during the day. Nelson, you have evening duty for this week. You can leave at midnight. Morgan, you're in charge of days this weekend. Ross, you'll take the evenings. If anything changes or I think we need to make adjustments, I'll let you know. I'd like a report on my desk from you all an hour after your shift is finished." They each nodded their agreement, and then, Marcus and all but Benson headed outside.

He stopped outside and looked up to the window of Abigail Connors's room. Marcus had had many a client stay in the same hotel and knew right where to look. He and his men were all going in different directions, and Marcus's long strides took him straight to the telegraph office, where he sent a telegram to Jacob Connors to let him know his daughter had arrived in Hot Springs and settled in her hotel safely. All this would be much easier if there were long-distance lines between the two cities—but Eureka Springs didn't even have phone service yet.

After meeting Abigail Connors in person, Marcus could certainly see why Jacob wanted someone to watch over her. On first meeting, she seemed quite confident and independent, but looking into her eyes, Marcus could see a sadness and vulnerability that told him there was much more to her than first appeared. He fought the urge to go back and check on her; she would be safe with Benson. Instead, he went back to his office and looked over the telegrams he'd just picked up. Evidently, Luke was back in town because the agent reports had been sorted and put on his desk. Marcus looked them over and studied his scheduling for the rest of the week. Abigail Connors wasn't the only client he was responsible for, and he needed to check in with other agents before he could call it a night.

Through it all, in the back of his mind, he kept thinking about the beautiful woman in his care, and he couldn't help but wonder just who broke the engagement and why.

three

Abigail wasn't quite sure what to do with herself once Marcus Wellington left. She liked the rooms she'd been given. The small sitting room had a settee in front of a fireplace and a writing desk by the window. A nice round table sat in the center of the room, with two chairs on either side of it, where she supposed she could have breakfast if she didn't want to go to the dining room downstairs. The room was beautifully decorated in different shades of blues and greens and felt soothing to her.

Abigail went into the bedroom to find the same colors on the drapes at the windows and on the bed. It was a very nice room. She spotted her trunk and bags at the end of the bed and quickly realized that the desk clerk had not sent anyone up to help her yet. She found the electric bell that she'd been told rang through to the office about the time a knock sounded on the sitting room door.

It was the maid come to help her. The young woman smiled. "Good evening, ma'am. I've been sent to help you get settled in."

"Good. I'd just rung the bell to remind the clerk." Before Abigail could let her in and shut the door, the bellboy who'd brought her things was there. "You rang, ma'am?"

"I did. I suppose I should have waited five minutes longer. I don't need anything now, thank you."

"All right. Just ring again if you do decide you need anything."

"Thank you, I will." Abigail noticed that his parting smile seemed to be centered on the young maid waiting for Abigail's directions. She waved to the bellboy and turned to the maid. "Will you be on duty tomorrow?"

The young woman bobbed her head. "Yes, ma'am, I will."

"I'd like you to arrange for my frocks to be pressed, then."

"Yes, ma'am. I'll do that first thing tomorrow morning."

She opened the trunk first as it held all of her frocks, and she would need one to change into when she went to dinner. Even though the maid was helpful, Abigail wondered why she hadn't brought her housekeeper. Abigail wasn't used to doing things like this herself. Well, she wasn't exactly doing it by herself, but neither was she used to doing things like this at all.

But she had assured her parents that she was self-sufficient, and she was determined to be just that—no matter how inconvenient it was. They thought she couldn't look after herself as it was; otherwise, they wouldn't have hired Marcus Wellington's agency to keep an eye on her.

She shook out one of her favorite walking dresses and handed it to the maid to hang in the wardrobe. Then she brought out a dinner dress for the girl to hang beside it. It took over an hour just to get her trunk unpacked, and her stomach was beginning to rumble. "Thank you, Miss—what is your name?"

"My name is Bea, ma'am. It's short for Beatrice. Fielding is my last name."

"Well, Bea, my name is Abigail Connors. Do you work every day?"

The young maid shook her head. "No, ma'am. I've just been hired to fill in when the other maids are off work."

"What kind of work have you done?"

"I was personal maid for Mrs. Rothschild until she passed

away a few weeks back. I took care of her clothing and helped her with her hair. . .and was there when she needed me."

"Hmm," Abigail said. "When you have free time, perhaps I'll be able to use you to help me from time to time with my hair, to keep my frocks pressed, and to run errands. Would you be interested in doing that?"

"Oh yes, ma'am! I'd love to help you when I can."

"I'll need to check your references."

"Yes, ma'am. I understand. I can give you a list. Would you want it now, or is tomorrow soon enough?"

"Tomorrow will be fine."

"Thank you, ma'am."

"You are welcome." Abigail looked around at her baggage. The trunk was empty, and she thought she could manage her bags. "I'll finish this up myself. Just stop by tomorrow to see about getting the most wrinkled frocks pressed for me and to give me your references."

"I will. Have a good evening, Miss Connors."

"Thank you. You have a nice one, too."

After the maid left, Abigail checked her hair and pinched her cheeks. She was starving and didn't have the energy to change for just an hour. Normally, she never would have thought of having dinner in the same dress she'd been traveling in, but the freedom of not knowing anyone in town was very liberating. Tired as she was, all Abigail wanted to do was have a good supper and come back to her room.

She headed down to the dining room, and once there, she was shown to a table in an alcove and seated facing out into the room. She was quite pleased. It was out of the way enough that she wouldn't feel out of place eating alone, yet she could see other diners plainly so that she didn't feel quite so alone. The waiter handed her a menu, and she was impressed with the selection the hotel offered.

She chose the veal cutlets with brown sauce and riced potatoes. For dessert, she chose lemon pie. As she waited for her meal, she took in the luxurious decor and was quite happy with her selection of hotels. She didn't think any of the others in town could be any nicer.

From the soft murmur of voices and the gentle clink of silverware, the hotel's clientele seemed quite sophisticated and genteel. Abigail was not made to feel uncomfortable at all for being by herself, and for that, she was quite thankful. She did see a man across the way keep looking at her, but she had a feeling he was the agent hired to watch over her. She had the impression from meeting Marcus Wellington that he didn't do anything by half measure, and she was certain that he would have her watched no matter where she went outside her room. She was a little surprised by the comfort that thought gave her.

Abigail actually enjoyed her dinner. The meal was delicious and the service outstanding. Best of all, she was able to watch the other diners without worrying that they might be discussing her broken engagement. If they were discussing her at all, they might be wondering who she was, but as she was at a hotel and the other guests weren't from Hot Springs, they probably weren't thinking of her at all. There was something very freeing about that thought.

That the wealthy frequented Hot Springs was evident in the way the guests were dressed, and Abigail would be certain to dress in a like manner while she was at the hotel. But as no one knew her, she wasn't going to worry about wearing her traveling clothes this evening. Instead, she just let herself enjoy the meal and the comings and goings of the other guests.

❧

Marcus had supper at one of the restaurants down the street from the Arlington Hotel. He hadn't been able to get Abigail Connors off his mind all evening, and it bothered him a great deal that he was still thinking about her. At first, he told himself it was because she was a new client and he just wanted to make sure everything went well—as he would any other client.

But from the moment he'd first seen Abigail, he knew she would be no ordinary client. Maybe it was because she was Jacob's daughter, or maybe it was because she was alone here in Hot Springs and he felt even more responsibility for her. He didn't know. All he was certain of was that he'd been thinking of her ever since he left the hotel. In the back of his mind were all the questions he'd like answered. He wanted to know why her wedding had been called off and why she was traveling alone. Why did she feel the need to leave Eureka Springs? And why was he so interested in her?

Marcus chided himself. Probably his investigative personality had his mind working overtime—that was all. But when he left the restaurant in time to meet his agents as they switched shifts at eight o'clock, he had a feeling it was more than that.

Benson was in the lobby, waiting for Nelson, when Marcus arrived. He put down the paper he was reading when Marcus took a seat beside him. "How's it going?"

"It's been quiet. Miss Connors came down for dinner and just went back up about ten minutes ago."

"Hmm. I would have thought she might eat in her room tonight."

"No, sir. She came down and had a leisurely meal. She seemed interested in watching the people around her and appeared quite at ease at a table by herself."

Perhaps she was more confident and independent than her father thought she was. "Well, I'm glad she had a good evening and is safe and sound back in her room," Marcus said. "I'm not sure everything will be quite so calm in the days to come."

"Most likely not," Benson said. "In this line of work, it usually isn't." Nelson arrived just then, and Benson filled him in on the calm night.

"I could use some quiet time after the last client I was assigned to," Nelson said as he settled into the chair Benson had just vacated. It had the best view of the stairs and the front desk.

They all laughed. Nelson's last client had been a wealthy woman with three spoiled children. As it turned out, her husband had apparently hired the Wellington Agency to watch his children while his wife went to the bathhouses for relaxation. Marcus assured both men, "Don't worry. I've got that name on my never-again list."

"Good thing, 'cause I'd have to decline the opportunity to do it again," Nelson said.

"Can't say I'd blame you," Marcus said as he and Benson turned to leave. "Have a good night."

He and Benson parted ways just outside the hotel, and Marcus found himself looking up at Miss Connors's hotel window. He wondered what she thought of Hot Springs and what kind of mood she'd be in the next day. He couldn't deny that he was looking forward to finding out.

❧

By the time Abigail got back to her room, she was ready for a good night's rest. She climbed into bed and pulled up her covers, but it didn't take long before Abigail realized that she wasn't going to drift off into a peaceful sleep as she'd hoped.

In the dark of the night and alone in a strange place, she began to think about home and all she had lost in the last few weeks.

Abigail fought the sudden urge to cry, but the hot tears won and cascaded down her cheeks. Brushing them away with the back of her hand, Abigail turned over and crunched her pillow, but she couldn't turn off her thoughts. The past was over with, and she needed to get on with her future. She wasn't sure she could.

For so long, she'd felt guilty about her sister's death. . .and now she knew her niece blamed her for it as well. . .even though it hadn't been her fault. She truly had been trying to save Rose when she'd followed her up the stairs and grabbed her arm and tried to get her to come with her the day of the fire. When Rose pulled away, she lost her balance and fell down the stairs. It hadn't been Abigail's fault, yet she knew she would always feel she could have, should have done something else—only she didn't know what.

Rose had been determined to save her keepsakes, telling Abigail that she'd be right back. But even had Abigail left her alone and let her go, she wouldn't have gotten out in time. The result would have been the same, and Abigail still would have blamed herself. If there was anything she should feel guilty about that day, it was that she'd envied her sister and wanted the life she had, but she had never *ever* wished her gone. And she had truly tried to convince Rose to get out in time.

Deep down, Abigail knew all that, but she would never forget seeing her sister fall down the stairs, rushing to help, only to find that Rose was badly hurt. All she could do when Rose told her to get Natalie to safety was just that—and hope she'd have time to come back and get her sister out. But that wasn't to be. By the time she'd turned around, the house was in flames. Abigail shuddered, remembering that sight in vivid detail. She would never forget that day. What really broke her heart was that now her niece remembered that day, too, and she wasn't likely to forget it. And in Natalie's mind, Abigail was to blame.

Abigail wished she could change the past, but there was no way that could be done. And she had no one but herself to blame for the heartache. There was no keeping the tears back, and she began to sob for the past, for the present, and for the future she'd wished for but lost.

❧

Abigail didn't wake until midmorning, but she was relieved to have the night over with. Even after her tears had subsided, she'd tossed and turned. Now she washed her face and could only hope that some of the puffiness around her eyes would go down before she met the Wellingtons.

She was pleased when Bea kept her word and came to take her dresses to be pressed. Bea handed her the list of references and told her that she'd try to come back that afternoon to help with her hair. As it was past midmorning but she was still not very hungry, Abigail sent a lunch order of tea and the soup of the day down to the kitchen with Bea, to be sent up at noon.

Abigail finished unpacking the bags she'd been too exhausted to deal with the night before, quite pleased that she managed to do it all herself. The thought that she really was quite spoiled came to mind, but she didn't let it stay there long. She didn't much like the picture it gave of herself.

After she'd freshened up, she was pleased that her lunch arrived right on time, and she thought about the day ahead as she ate her split pea soup and enjoyed her pot of tea. She was looking forward to meeting the Wellingtons. She'd realized just how alone she was during her long night, and she would be glad to have someone to call on if needed. At least they were old friends of her parents, and she hoped that would make it easier to get to know them.

Bea brought her gowns up just after one o'clock and was able to stay and help with preparations for attending the Wellingtons' tea. She brushed Abigail's hair to a bright shine and then pulled it up, twisted and turned it, and pinned it on top of her head. Bea explained each step so that Abigail could attempt to do it herself if Bea wasn't available. The maid pulled a few curls out around Abigail's face, and Abigail was very pleased with the results.

"Thank you, Bea. I'll try to do it myself tomorrow morning for church."

"I'm sure you'll be able to. Just brush, pull up, and twist."

"I think that sounds easier than it is, but I'll try." After all, she was going to be here awhile. She wasn't going to have someone at her disposal all the time. She thought of hiring a personal maid—after all, many people traveled with their personal staff. Somehow that only reinforced the fact that she *was* very spoiled, and for some reason, she didn't want the Wellingtons to see her that way.

Bea helped her into a visiting dress, a pale blue crepe de chine draped to the side and trimmed with gold embroidery. By the time Bea left, Abigail thought she looked as nice as she could.

Marcus Wellington arrived promptly at three, and when Abigail opened the door to him, she was a little surprised at how nervous she was.

"Good afternoon, Miss Connors. It is a lovely day out. Are you ready to go?"

"It is, Mr. Wellington. And I am ready and looking forward to meeting your parents." She gathered her parasol, reticule, and key. After locking the door, she dropped it in her small bag and took the arm Marcus held out to her as they went downstairs to the lobby.

He led her out to a surrey with a fringed canopy top, helped her in, and then rounded the vehicle to take his own seat. With a flick of his wrist, they were off, down Central Avenue back toward the train depot. Abigail quite enjoyed the ride while Marcus pointed out several businesses to her. A general store owned by a Mr. E. Burgauer was said to have a varied stock, and according to Marcus, the William J. Little Grocery at the junction of Central and Reserve was one of the largest in the city.

He also pointed out the post office and Cooper and Johnston's Stationery and Bookstore. A photographer and a large jewelry store occupied the same block. And they passed several banks, too. There was so much to look at—and Abigail was seeing just part of the town. She looked forward to learning her way around.

Marcus turned off Central Avenue and made several more turns before he stopped the surrey at a large home on a quiet street. He tied the reins to the hitching post at the street and helped her down. Before they got halfway to the house, the door was thrown open and a woman who reminded Abigail of her own mother stepped out onto the wide porch. "Marcus, dear, don't dawdle. Bring Miss Connors inside— I've been waiting all day to meet her."

When Abigail stepped up onto the porch, Mrs. Wellington gave her a quick hug. "I am so glad to finally meet you, dear. You look just like your mother at your age! Isn't she lovely, Marcus?"

four

Abigail held her breath, waiting for Marcus Wellington's answer to his mother's question.

"Yes, Mother, she is very lovely. And she's been looking forward to meeting you and Father, too, so let's get her inside out of the heat."

Abigail felt the color rise up her neck and onto her cheeks. She wondered if Marcus was just being polite or if he was being sincere. She had a feeling he was uncomfortable in having to answer his mother's question. But Mrs. Wellington paid no attention and pulled Abigail inside the large foyer.

"Your father is in his study; would you go get him, Marcus? We'll be waiting in the parlor," Mrs. Wellington said. She led Abigail over to the right and into a parlor that made her feel right at home. It was so much like her parents' parlor that her mother could have decorated it. Obviously, the two women had similar tastes.

"Please, dear, take a seat anywhere," Mrs. Wellington said, sitting on the burgundy-colored settee. A tea tray laden with all kinds of sandwiches and sweet treats rested on the round table in front of her. "I'll pour tea as soon as Marcus and his father join us. I can't tell you how pleased I am that you are here. I'm hoping that your parents will pay us a visit soon. Although we keep letters going back and forth, it's been much too long since we've seen them in person."

Marcus and his father entered the room, and Abigail could see that Marcus looked very much like Mr. Wellington. They both had that engaging dimple when they smiled.

"Well now, how pretty you are," the older Mr. Wellington said as he came over and took Abigail's hand in his. "You do look like your mother. We are so glad you are here in Hot Springs and we have this chance to meet you. You were only a child the last time we saw you."

Abigail couldn't remember actually meeting them, so she must have been young.

"I'm very pleased to meet you all, too, Mr. Wellington. My parents think of you as among their closest and dearest friends."

Mrs. Wellington poured their tea, and Marcus handed round a tray with delicate sandwiches and little iced tea cakes. The afternoon passed pleasantly with the Wellingtons telling her stories about her parents when they were all younger. When it was time to leave, Abigail hated to depart. The evening loomed long and lonely to her.

"We'd love to have you join us for church tomorrow and for dinner here afterward, if you would be so inclined," Mrs. Wellington invited.

Abigail didn't hesitate to accept. "I would love to. Thank you for the invitation!"

"Wonderful! Marcus will pick you up in the morning, then, won't you, dear?"

"I'll be happy to," Marcus answered.

For a moment, Abigail's heart skipped a beat. Then she remembered that he was actually working for her father and escorting her would be part of his job. Still, she managed a smile. "I'll be ready. Thank you again for the invitation, Mrs. Wellington."

"You are quite welcome, dear. We are looking forward to introducing you to our church family and others in town. We really are quite excited about having you here."

The older Wellingtons followed them out onto the porch, and Abigail waved to them as she left. She dreaded the long evening awaiting her back at the hotel after Marcus dropped her off.

Once they were on their way, Abigail turned to Marcus and said, "Your parents are wonderful, Mr. Wellington. They made me feel very welcome. Thank you for taking me."

"They felt the same about you. I could tell," Marcus replied. And his parents did. It was obvious that they liked Abigail Connors from the first. Perhaps it was because she was their good friends' daughter, but he had a feeling his parents would have taken to Abigail even if she weren't. "Thank you for going to see them."

"I'm glad I did—and that I get to see them again. Are you sure you don't mind picking me up and taking me to church—"

"Of course not. I'll be happy to. I'd be—"

"Oh yes," Abigail interrupted. "I'd almost forgotten you are being paid—"

"Miss Connors, I'd be happy to take you to church even if your father hadn't hired my agency to protect you while you are here." Marcus had a feeling that he knew what she was thinking and wanted to assure her. "I will be more than glad to take you to church and back to my parents' home for Sunday dinner."

She was silent for a moment, and then she said, "Thank you. I will be ready."

"Good." Marcus hoped that she'd seen she was more than just a client to him. "Since there is that family connection, do you think we might be able to call each other by our first names?" He grinned at her, hoping for a smile.

"I suppose we could. It would certainly be easier if we are

to see much of each other while I am here."

"Oh, we're going to see each other, Abigail—aside from the fact that my firm is in charge of protecting you, you are also a friend of the family."

"Then we can go by first names. Marcus it will be."

He liked the way she said his name.

"Well then, Abigail, would you care to have dinner at your hotel with me tonight?"

"Marcus, you don't have to watch me every waking hour."

"I know that. The invitation wasn't part of the job. We both have to eat, and I often eat at the Arlington. The food is excellent." They arrived at the hotel just then, and the topic was dropped for the time being. Marcus, however, had every intention of getting back to it.

He helped Abigail down from the buggy and walked her inside the hotel. But before he saw her to her room, he took hold of her arm and steered her toward Morgan, who'd come into the hotel just ahead of them. Marcus had let him know earlier that he could take a few hours off. Now he was sitting in a chair that had a good view of the staircase, reading—or pretending to read—a paper.

"Morgan, I thought Miss Connors should meet the men I have assigned to her. Miss Connors, this is Alan Morgan. He is on day duty this weekend."

"How do you do, Miss Connors? Be assured that if you need anything, I'll be right here."

"Thank you, Mr. Morgan. I'm glad to know who you are and that I can call on you if needed."

"Anytime, ma'am." The agent bowed at the waist.

"Your relief will be here shortly, Morgan, and I'll be talking to you later."

"Yes, sir," Morgan said. He went back to his paper as

Marcus led Abigail away.

He accompanied her up to her room and took the key from her. After unlocking the door and giving a look inside, he handed the key back to her. "You know, you never answered me. Will you have supper with me? We both have to eat, and while those little sandwiches my mother served are delicious, they didn't do much to fill me up." He looked down at her with a grin.

"I'd like to change first. Can you wait for me to do that?"

She looked up into his eyes, and Marcus felt something he'd never experienced before. He wasn't even sure what it was. He only knew he badly wanted her to say yes, and he'd wait for however long it took.

"I can. Will an hour be enough time?" He'd wait longer if needed.

"Yes, I can be ready by then."

"I'll be back up to get you"—Marcus looked at his watch—"at seven o'clock."

"I'll be ready."

He nodded and turned to leave, grinning as he did so. He didn't have much time either, if he was going to change and get back by seven.

❧

Abigail was extremely proud that she'd managed to get ready with five minutes to spare before Marcus would be knocking on her door. Thanks to Bea's help earlier that day, her hair still looked quite nice. And due to Bea, all of her frocks were pressed and ready to choose from, so it made an easy time of it for Abigail. Thankfully, she didn't have to change undergarments, and she chose a dress of peach satin with a brown overskirt that draped to the back. She'd just finished putting on her jewelry when Marcus arrived.

From the look in his eyes, she felt she looked quite presentable.

"You look lovely." He smiled into her eyes. "And I am starving. Are you ready?"

"Yes, I am. And I'm a little hungry, too."

"I told you those little sandwiches don't fill one up. Let's go." He took the key from her and locked the door behind them before handing it back to her. She took the arm he offered, and they descended the stairs and walked to the dining room.

Abigail had thought she'd been treated well the night before, but evidently coming in with a gentleman did gain one a higher level of service. Or perhaps it was because of the man she was with. Marcus seemed to garner respect wherever he went. She'd noticed it from the train depot to the hotel clerk and bellboys, and now—here at the restaurant. They were seated at a table in front of the windows, where Abigail could be seen as well as see most of the other diners in the room. She took the seat the waiter held out for her and glanced around. Satisfied that she was dressed in a similar style to the other women in the room, she felt herself relax, only briefly letting herself wonder why it mattered more tonight than it had the night before.

They looked over the menus the waiter had left. "I had the veal last night, and it was delicious, but I'd like to try something different tonight."

"I can recommend the filet of beef with scalloped potatoes and brown sauce," Marcus said. "It is one of my favorite dishes."

Abigail scanned the menu before nodding her head. "I'll try that, then. Do you really eat here often?"

"I do—several times a week, in fact. It's near my apartment and office."

"You don't eat at your parents'?" Abigail was curious about this man who'd been hired to protect her.

"Of course I do. But many times I am working late or in a hurry, and it's easier to eat out."

The waiter came back to the table, and while Marcus gave him their order, she was able to look at Marcus without his knowing. He looked quite handsome in his black wool suit and crisp white shirt. She could feel the color creep up her face when he looked back to see her watching him, and she quickly turned her head and looked out the window while he finished their order.

She liked Hot Springs at night. The streetlights made it easy to see who was out and about, and she felt almost as safe as when she was at home in Eureka Springs. But was that because of the lighting outside or the man across from her? She knew. Much as she didn't want to admit it—and sometimes resented it—part of her was glad that Marcus Wellington was in charge of her safety.

"What time do you want to start checking out the bath-houses on Monday?" Marcus asked once the waiter left the table.

"I thought around ten in the morning." Abigail had slept in that day, but normally, even if she was up late the night before, she was a fairly early riser. And even if she weren't, she wouldn't want Marcus Wellington to think she was lazy. After all, she'd promised her father that she would check into things for him, and he would want to think she was acting in a professional way.

"That should be a good time. If not, I'm sure you can set up appointments with the managers for another time."

"That is true. It isn't as if I have to do it all in one day." After all, she had no intention of going back home anytime soon.

Their first course of cream of asparagus soup arrived, and while they ate, Marcus pointed out several people he knew. Actually, it was more than several; it seemed he knew most of the people in the dining room. She supposed it was no different than when she was out in Eureka Springs. She'd been born and raised there, and while she knew many people, she couldn't recall ever being treated with such open respect and friendliness as she'd seen Marcus treated with. It wasn't a thought she wanted to explore—not at the moment anyway—and she was relieved when the waiter brought the next course and broke into her thoughts.

The filet of beef was the most tender she'd ever eaten, and she was glad Marcus had suggested it. "This is wonderful. I can see why it is one of your favorites."

"I'm glad you like it. Thank you for agreeing to have dinner with me. It's nice to have company."

Abigail had a feeling he could have company any time he wanted, but she didn't say so. "You are welcome. I don't really like eating alone, either." *Now why did I say that?* Marcus didn't need to know that.

"I'm sure you don't have to do it often. And once you meet people here, you won't need to anymore. I'm sure you'll have invitations from many people and keep me quite busy."

"What do you mean?"

"I will be the one accompanying you most of where you go while you are here."

"I'm sure you have more important things to do. I assumed you'd assign one of your agents to watch me."

"I thought about it, but I've decided to do that myself. You are the daughter of the man who helped me start my business. My father makes a good living, but I didn't want to take money that he might need in his own business. Your father loaned me money when no one else would. . .not to mention that he is an old family friend. And I'm sure that by the time you leave Hot Springs, you will be considered a family friend in your own right."

While Abigail hoped he was right—she really liked his parents and could see why her parents regarded them so highly—she reminded herself that in escorting her around town, Marcus would only be doing the job her father was paying him to do. That thought dampened her mood somewhat, and she was glad that their dessert of orange and cream coconut cake was served so that she didn't have to talk—but she found she'd lost her appetite. She mostly pushed the cake around on her plate until she looked up to find Marcus watching her.

"Are you all right? This cake is delicious, and you've barely touched it."

He really had the most brilliantly blue eyes Abigail had ever seen, and looking into them did funny things to her heart. "I guess I'm still a little tired from the travel and all."

"That is understandable. Would you like some coffee or tea before we leave?"

"No, thank you. I've asked for tea to be brought to my room each night before bedtime. It helps me sleep better." At least it usually did. Abigail hoped it would settle her down tonight and make her sleepy. She didn't want another night like the last one.

Marcus motioned the waiter over and paid for their meal.

"You don't have to pay for mine. They can put it on my hotel bill."

Marcus shook his head as the waiter left the table. "No. I asked you to have dinner with me." He got up and pulled out her chair.

As Marcus guided her through the dining room, they were stopped several times by diners who knew him, and he made sure to introduce her to the people at each table. By the time they left the dining room, she knew she'd never remember all their names; Marcus knew them all, and she'd just have to count on him to remind her.

He walked her to her room and, after taking her key, unlocked the door. "Wait here." He entered, and Abigail assumed he was checking the room to make sure no one was there. When he came out, he handed the key back to her. "Everything is fine. I hope you sleep well."

She took the key and was surprised when an electric spark shot up her arm at the brief touch of his fingertips against hers. "I—thank you for dinner. It was delicious."

"You are welcome. Thank you for putting up with my company." He grinned at her, and that dimple at the corner of his mouth seemed to deepen as he looked down at her.

She couldn't help but smile back. "It was nice to have company. What time should I be ready in the morning?"

"I'll be here to pick you up at nine o'clock."

"I'll be ready." *I did it today; surely I can do it tomorrow.*

Marcus gave a little salute and turned to leave. "It looks as if your pot of tea is arriving."

Sure enough, a bellboy was bringing her tea tray. Marcus waited until he set it down on the table in Abigail's sitting room and left. Then he turned to Abigail again. "You sleep well. I'll see you in the morning."

She nodded and stepped inside the room. "I'll see you then."

"Lock the door. I won't leave until you do."

"All right." Abigail stepped inside and shut the door. Then she turned the key in the lock and wondered if he was waiting to hear the click it made.

"Good girl. Good night, Abigail."

"Good night, Marcus."

It was only when she crossed the room and took out her earrings while looking in the mirror that she realized she was smiling. She moved to the side of the window and pulled the drapes aside just a bit to look down at the street, wondering if Marcus was still in the hotel talking to the agent who was in the lobby that night or if he'd already left.

She watched for a moment longer until a man who looked to be about Marcus's size walked out. From the gaslight below, she was pretty sure it was he, and when he turned and looked up, her heart did a flip. Was he looking up at her room? She quickly dropped the drape and moved away from the window. Even though she didn't think he could see her looking out, she wanted to be sure.

She poured her tea and sipped, thinking back over the evening. If she had to be protected, she supposed it could be worse. Marcus was actually very easy to be around—not to mention how entertaining it was to watch for that dimple. *All in all, maybe it won't be so bad having someone to watch over me.* Especially since Marcus had decided he would be the one to escort her around town.

વ

Marcus walked outside the hotel and didn't try to stop himself from looking up at the windows of Abigail's room. Watching over her was his job, after all. The light still glowed, and he imagined her sipping her tea. Was she thinking back over the evening?

He hoped she enjoyed herself as much as he did. It had been a treat to have such a lovely woman sitting across from him for dinner. Most of the time, he ate alone, and he'd found Abigail to be quite captivating as a dinner companion.

She seemed to want to come across as tough and independent, but he had a feeling she was anything but. Something in the expression in her eyes made him want to know more about her—something that reached out to him in a way he'd never experienced before.

He felt protective of her, and this feeling had absolutely nothing to do with the fact that her father had hired him to do just that. He wanted to know what it was that made her look so vulnerable and why her wedding had been called off. Perhaps it was time to find out more than what Jacob had told him. Marcus felt an urgent need to know all he could about Abigail Connors because she was quickly becoming more than just a client to him.

He headed home, determined to find out all he could about her and looking more than a little forward to the next day. While he walked, he prayed that the Lord would help Abigail with whatever it was that made her look so sad when she thought no one was watching her.

five

Abigail was proud of herself the next morning. She managed to put her hair up the way Bea had explained to her, and she was dressed in her favorite Sunday dress when Marcus picked her up for the ride to church.

His parents were waiting for them, and while Mr. Wellington greeted her by clasping her hand in his, Mrs. Wellington gave her a hug as soon as Abigail turned to her. Then she took over from Marcus and led her into the church. From the moment Abigail entered the church, she felt at home.

Mrs. Wellington introduced her as they made their way to a pew near the front of the building. Over and over again, Mrs. Wellington said, "Please meet Abigail Connors, the daughter of dear friends of ours in Eureka Springs." She'd give the parishioners' names, too, and Abigail could only hope she would remember some of them. As she took her seat beside Mrs. Wellington, she realized that she hadn't been to church since she'd broken her engagement to Nate. She couldn't face having to explain everything to the people she'd gone to church with all her life.

Now she wondered why. Had she been afraid that they'd be talking about her behind their hymnals? Or that they might be thinking that the broken engagement was what she deserved? She'd known those people all her life, yet. . . had she really? As the service got underway with prayer and singing, Abigail realized that through the years she'd gone to church more because it was expected of her than because she wanted to be there. . .needed to be there. *Oh, dear Lord, please forgive me. Please help me to become the child You want me to be, and please forgive me for putting everything else in front of You.*

Abigail blinked back tears and hoped that no one noticed. She'd been so concerned with herself she couldn't even remember the last time she'd prayed. Nor could she really recall listening to a sermon all the way through. But today was different, and she found herself holding on to every word the minister was saying about forgiveness of others and one's self. She was beginning to realize that she had much to ask forgiveness for.

She was still thinking about the sermon when the service ended and she and Marcus followed his parents back to their home. Mrs. Wellington's dining table was set with fine china and crystal—for twelve. Before Abigail had a chance to become nervous, several of the people she had been introduced to earlier arrived, and she strived to remember their names. The minister and his wife arrived last, and everyone seemed to want to talk to Abigail.

"We are so glad to meet you, Miss Connors," a man she'd been introduced to earlier said. "I've heard wonderful things about your family. How long are you planning on staying in Hot Springs?"

"I'm not certain. I'm looking into some things for my father." Abigail spoke the truth. She was going to do as requested, and she had no idea when she was going home. No time soon— that was for sure.

"Would you happen to know the Joneses? They are dear friends of ours and moved to Eureka Springs a couple of years ago."

"No, I don't believe I've met them. It's possible my parents would know them, though." Abigail felt faint for a moment. If they knew people in Eureka Springs, it was possible they'd heard about her wedding being called off and had heard any number of things about her.

"We'd love to have you to dinner one evening soon," his wife said.

Her tone was very nice and friendly, and Abigail tried to put her fears to the back of her mind. "Why, thank you." At least it would get her out, and she supposed she should get to know some of the people in town. It might be that she would be staying for quite some time. Abigail just wished she could remember their names. "That would be lovely."

"I'll send you an invitation this next week, then."

"I look forward to it." She was going to have to ask Marcus who the couple was, because hard as she tried, she couldn't recall their names.

But she did remember the next person who came up to her and asked if she'd be free for lunch during the next week. Abigail had been introduced to the young woman and her husband before church—and recalled that her name was Sally Monroe.

"I'm certain I will be available," Abigail said. Sally appeared to be about her age, and she was quite nice. "I'd love to have lunch."

"How about Tuesday? I could meet you at your hotel, and we could have lunch there."

"That should work fine." They set a time, and Abigail found herself looking forward to getting to know Sally better. She didn't really miss her friends in Eureka Springs as much as she thought she might. And that, too, was strange to her for she saw some of them almost every day.

Mrs. Wellington called everyone to the table, and Abigail

wasn't disappointed to find herself sitting next to Marcus. He'd almost disappeared into the background while others had come up to speak to her. Now he leaned near and whispered, "How are you doing?"

"I'm fine. I just wish I could remember that couple right across from us."

"They are the Bransons: Peter and Emily." His voice was low and for her ears only.

"Oh, thank you. They want me to come to dinner soon."

"You'll enjoy yourself. They are very nice people."

As the meal progressed, they all seemed to go out of their way to make Abigail feel welcome in their town. The minister and his wife were very nice, also.

"We're very glad you joined us today. It's sometimes hard to go to church when you are away from home."

Abigail didn't want to admit that there'd been times at home when it had been hard for her to go. "Your church has a very good feeling to it. Everyone was very friendly and welcoming."

"We hope you'll join us again."

"I'm planning on it."

The afternoon passed quickly. After dinner, they played a game of croquet in the big, shady backyard, and Abigail enjoyed herself immensely. After everyone else had left, the Wellingtons insisted that she stay for a light supper, and by the time Marcus took her back to the hotel that evening, she didn't feel quite so alone in a new town.

He walked her to her room and, after checking inside, joined her just outside the door once more. "What time do you want me to pick you up tomorrow? Didn't we decide on around ten?"

His smile showed his dimple, and as Abigail looked into

those blue eyes, her heart fluttered against her ribs. "Yes, we did. I'll be ready."

"Good."

"I'm sure you've had second thoughts about telling my father you'd be responsible for me. Between doing what you've been hired to do and doing what your family expects you to do, you certainly have your work cut out for you."

He leaned against the door frame and looked into her eyes. "Yes, ma'am, I believe I do."

The look in his eyes kept her from taking offense.

He shoved himself away from the door frame and gave her a push. "Lock up. Sleep well, and I'll see you in the morning."

"See you then," Abigail breathed as she backed into her room. She shut the door and turned the key.

"Good night," Marcus said from the other side.

She could hear him walk away as she whispered, "Good night."

❧

Marcus walked out of the hotel after he'd had a word with Morgan and Ross, who were changing shifts. Abigail didn't know just how true her words were. He certainly did have his work cut out for him. . .and the biggest part of it was making sure he didn't begin to care too much for his client.

He'd watched her this afternoon at his parents'. She wasn't nearly as confident as she would like everyone to think she was. And she seemed a little. . .apprehensive, especially when the Bensons had first gone up to talk to her. She'd turned quite pale for a moment. He wondered why. There was so much he didn't know about Abigail Connors, and the more he was around her, the more he wanted to know about her. He'd put a man on it first thing tomorrow.

Marcus glanced up at her window and fought the urge to

wait until her lights went out before heading for home. He had an agent there in case she needed anything, and he'd see her the next day. He chuckled and shook his head. Abigail Connors was taking up entirely too many of his thoughts.

ఇ

Abigail was glad to see Bea early the next morning. She'd washed her hair and needed the maid's help in making herself presentable. Bea also gathered the gowns that needed to be pressed and the other garments that needed to be washed and took them down to the hotel laundry for Abigail.

"Thank you, Bea," Abigail said as the young woman put her hair up for her.

"You are welcome, Miss Connors. I'm glad to do it. I talked to the manager, and he said that if you need me to help you on my days off, I could. So just let me know what you might want me to do for you and what time you need me. One of the regulars who'd taken a month's leave is back, and I'll only be working on Tuesdays and Thursdays now."

"Oh, well that will work out wonderfully for me. What are you being paid for your day here?"

Bea told her, and Abigail nodded. "I'll pay you that for each day you come to help me out. I'd like you on Saturday mornings and the weekday mornings that you aren't working. If I need you to help me get ready for a special evening function, do you think you could do that?"

"Of course! I'd be happy to." Bea's smile was wide.

"Good. I've been able to make myself presentable, but I have to admit that I've missed my housekeeper. She always helped me get ready to go out. I'm hoping to learn more from you so that I can manage on my own better."

"I'll be glad to help," Bea said. "It's really not that hard. You'll do fine."

Her sweetness touched Abigail. It was nice to hear encouraging words, even if they were from someone she barely knew—and a maid at that. Not normally one to exchange small talk with servants, Abigail surprised herself by confiding in the young woman, "Thank you, Bea. I hope so. But I'm afraid I've been quite spoiled."

By the time Marcus came to pick her up to visit the bathhouses, Abigail felt she looked very nice. She'd chosen a blue-and-brown-plaid walking dress, accessorized with a blue hat and parasol. Bea had arranged little curls to peek out from under the hat on Abigail's forehead, and she felt quite stylish when Marcus arrived.

He looked quite nice and professional in his suit and bowler. Seeing that dimple flash as he smiled gave her that fluttery feeling again, and she wasn't sure she welcomed it. She wasn't even sure what it meant as she'd never experienced it before.

"You look very nice this morning," he said as they went downstairs. "Have you decided which bathhouse you want to visit first?"

She shook her head. "I thought maybe we'd just start out from here and visit the closest one first."

"That sounds good to me. It's a lovely day out. Would you like to walk?"

They stepped outside. Noting the blue, cloudless sky, Abigail nodded. "Yes, let's. It will be easier than getting in and out of a buggy, anyway."

Marcus chuckled. "That's what I thought. Besides, this way you can see more of the city up close."

Abigail did feel a little nervous as she and Marcus set out for the first bathhouse. This was the first time her father had ever sent her to look into any kind of business venture for him, and she wanted to make him proud. "What is the difference between the springs at home and the ones here in Hot Springs?" she asked as Marcus took her arm and steered her out onto the walk.

"They are totally different. The springs here are hot." He grinned down at her. "Hence the name of the town. The springs in Eureka Springs are not hot. They are known for what many believe to be their mineral healing properties. Our springs start out at around 143 degrees and have to be cooled before they can be used in the bathhouses. Many people who have suffered from ailments have found that the hot waters have helped them. Others come because they think the hot baths are good for them and that they make them feel better."

They arrived at the Big Iron Bathhouse first, and after introducing herself to the receptionist, Abigail asked if she could make an appointment.

"For a bath? My dear, look around you. We have several people waiting now. No, we cannot accommodate you now."

"No, I don't want a bath. I'd like to make an appointment to tour the facility."

"You mean you don't want a bath? You just want to look around?"

"That's right." Abigail didn't feel she needed to explain any more than that.

"Well, I'm not sure. You'd have to talk to the manager about that."

"That's what I'm wanting to do. Is he in?"

"No. He won't be back until this afternoon."

Abigail didn't want to lose her temper with Marcus standing right beside her. "All right. May I make an appointment for tomorrow?"

The receptionist looked at her book. "He can probably see

you this time tomorrow."

"That will be fine. Please put me down for that." She handed her a business card her father had made for her, calling her a representative of the Connors Bank of Eureka Springs. "Please tell him I am representing my father's bank."

The receptionist's tone quickly changed. "I'll be glad to, Miss Connors. We'll see you tomorrow."

The lobby had been somewhat dim, and Abigail opened her parasol against the brightness of the light outside.

"You handled that very well."

"Thank you. She wasn't very helpful, was she?"

Marcus chuckled. "Not until she found out your father is a banker." He shook his head. "It always bothers me when people are treated differently depending on their circumstances or how they look. I guess that is why I think so much of your father. When I went in, he didn't know that I was the grown son of his good friends. I didn't want that to be a factor in whether or not he gave me a loan."

"He is a very special man." It suddenly struck Abigail that the deferential treatment she'd always received had been more because of her father and his position in town rather than anything she'd ever done. She wondered why she'd never really thought about it before. Deep down she knew the truth, but had she thought it was her right to be treated so well just because her father was so well thought of—or because of how wealthy he was? If so, how impertinent of her.

They were at the next bathhouse before she had time to reflect further, and Abigail was relieved. She didn't much like the turn her thoughts had taken. The Old Hale Bathhouse was nicer than its name implied, probably because it had been renovated.

"There are regulations and inspections on a regular basis.

If the government decides improvements need to be made, they are made. Otherwise, their licenses can be taken away," Marcus explained.

The manager was available, and he showed her what he could while they waited for one of the rooms and a tub to be cleaned so that she could see that. "When bathers come in, their valuables are given to us, and we put them in our safe," the manager explained. "Then they are provided with fresh sheets and towels. The towels are to dry off with after the bath, and the sheets are to wrap in for the rubdown. The bathers provide their own mitts and bathrobes. An attendant oversees the bath. The tubs are scrubbed clean after every bath, and the rooms cleaned and readied for the next bather."

"And how long does the bathing take?" Abigail asked.

"Around twenty minutes, a little more or less, depending on the bather."

They toured the facility and then saw the room that had just been cleaned. The marble room had a stall.

"The stall is at about 150 degrees, and the baths are at 98 degrees," the manager explained. "Obviously, going from one to the other creates a kind of shock to the body, but it is what invigorates our clients—once they've perspired out the impurities, relaxed in the bath, and been rubbed down by our attendants."

By the time they arrived back at the front desk, they'd seen several people emerge from their rooms, some looking invigorated and others quite drained.

"I assure you that those who look a bit the worse for it will be feeling totally different after a rest."

Abigail certainly hoped so. She might be looking into this business venture for her father, but after this morning, she had no intention of trying it out for herself. She thanked the manager for his time, and she and Marcus walked out into the bright sunshine.

"Do you want to go to the next bathhouse, or would you like to take time for lunch?" Marcus asked. "There is a restaurant down the street a little ways that I think you'd enjoy."

"Yes, I think I'd like that. Thank you. I feel a little drained myself."

"It's because of the heat and the humidity inside the bathhouses. There's no way to get around that."

"I suppose not, with the water so hot. I don't think I realized just how. . .muggy it would feel inside one of those rooms."

Marcus led her farther down the street to a small restaurant, and Abigail breathed a sigh of relief that it felt cool inside. After looking over the menu, she chose a French salad, a cup of bouillon, and tea.

After the waiter left, Marcus turned to her. "We have several more bathhouses. Do you want to continue to visit them today?"

"Maybe one more, if we can see the manager. The rest can wait until tomorrow or the next day. I'm sure you have other things to do."

Marcus looked at her and shook his head. "Whatever else I might need to do can be worked around you."

"But—"

"Abigail, are you trying to get rid of me?"

His dimple flashed, and her heartbeat sped up. "No, of course not. Besides, I know that if I should go anywhere without your knowledge, one of your agents will be right behind me."

"I'm glad you realize that. It will make me worry a little less when I'm not there."

"Then I take it that I *can* leave the hotel should I need to do some shopping?"

"Of course you can. I don't want you to feel as if you are a prisoner, and I'm certain that's the last thing your father intended when he asked me to make sure you are safe while you are here."

"Good." Abigail found herself smiling at him. "I'm glad you realize that."

Marcus threw back his head and laughed. "I think we are beginning to understand each other. I will be accompanying you to any events you may want to attend, though. Parties, the opera—that kind of thing. We need to be clear on that."

Somehow the idea of him escorting her only gave her a warm feeling and a sense of safety. "We're clear. I suppose you need to know that I've hired one of the part-time maids to work for me on her off days. And should I go out to the post office or shopping, she will most likely accompany me."

"I'd like to have her credentials checked out."

"All right. I'll get them to you. She seems very nice and has been quite helpful to me. I'm sure she will check out just fine."

"In the business I'm in, I've found you can never be too sure. I hope she does check out."

Abigail did, too. While she didn't want to go home, she was used to a life filled with friends and family. To her surprise, she even missed her housekeeper. Abigail had confided in her from time to time, and although she never really asked for her opinion, still she was someone to talk to. Now, Abigail found that she did miss all that. She liked Bea and was looking forward to have someone to talk to when she wasn't with Marcus or his family.

And she was relieved that she would be able to come and

go from the hotel for more than one reason. She didn't want to count on Marcus for everything. She'd looked forward to seeing him much too much today, and she didn't welcome that feeling. . .not at all.

six

Abigail gave Bea's references to Marcus when he came to pick her up the next day to visit several other bathhouses on her list.

He handed the papers to the agent. . .she believed his name was Nelson. She'd been introduced to him the day before, but because Marcus had someone at the hotel nearly twenty-four hours a day, she was still a bit confused on who was who.

Bea had helped her get ready for the day, and Abigail felt confident that she looked her best. She found that because she was doing business for her father, she wanted to look professional, not just for her sake, but for his as well.

"You are awfully quiet this morning. Are you all right?" Marcus asked as they started down the street.

"I'm fine, thank you. I forgot to tell you that I'm meeting Sally Monroe at the hotel for lunch at noon. She'd asked me about it at your parents', and I had a note reminding me of it first thing this morning."

"I'll be sure to have you back in plenty of time. We can visit one or two bathhouses this morning and another this afternoon or tomorrow. But before I forget, my mother wondered if you'd have dinner with us on Saturday evening."

Abigail had been wondering when she would see Mr. and Mrs. Wellington again and was quite happy to receive the invitation. "I'd love to."

"Good. I'll let her know." He gripped her elbow as he accompanied her inside the Big Iron Bathhouse. After a quick tour of its facilities, they agreed they had time to visit the Independent Bathhouse. Marcus led Abigail up to the reception desk.

"Good morning, can we see the manager, please?" Marcus asked.

"I'll see if I can find him. Please have a seat." It was apparent that the young woman was attracted to Marcus by the smile on her face. She appeared to be about Abigail's age. When she got up to go find the manager, Abigail could see that she was a bit taller. She had dark hair and brown eyes and was quite pretty. Abigail couldn't help but wonder if the young woman and Marcus knew each other—and then she wondered if he was courting anyone.

Knowing it really wasn't any of her business and trying to ignore a little niggle of jealousy at the thought that he might, Abigail turned and looked around the foyer. "This is nice. All the bathhouses seem to be a bit different inside, but I suppose it is that and the way each are managed that draw in different people."

"That is true. The city also has a free bathhouse for those who can't afford to come to the nicer ones."

"Oh? I didn't know that."

"With Hot Springs being inside the National Reservation, and even though it has its own city government, the federal government oversees the springs and anything to do with them."

"I see. Papa will have to take that under consideration, too."

"Yes, he will. I can set up an appointment with the park superintendent, if you'd like. He can tell you all you'll need to know."

"I might need to do that. I'll let you know." Hard as she tried, Abigail couldn't keep the coolness out of her tone, and she wasn't sure why it was there.

When Marcus raised an eyebrow and looked at her questioningly, she realized he'd heard it, too.

She quickly added, "I need to check with Papa, first. Then if he thinks I need to meet with the superintendent, I'll ask you to make an appointment."

"Good enough," was all Marcus said.

The receptionist returned, and Abigail caught the smile that passed between her and Marcus. She didn't like it, and more. . .she didn't like that she didn't like it. What was wrong with her? This man had been hired by her father to make sure she was safe. He was the son of dear friends of her parents. That was all. She and Marcus had no relationship, and she wasn't looking for one. Not after loving someone for as long as she'd loved Nate and then to have it all for naught. No. She didn't need to think along those lines.

The receptionist turned to her. "Mr. Martin asked if you could come back a little later. He's showing a prospective client around."

"That's all right." Abigail wasn't sure she wanted to come back. At least not soon. And possibly not with Marcus. "I'll check back or make an appointment for another time."

"We can make an appointment now, if you'd like. That would probably be best," the young woman said.

She was being nice, and Abigail didn't want to appear rude—especially not in front of Marcus. "Can we make it for around three today?"

The receptionist consulted her appointment book and nodded. "Yes, he is free at that time."

"We'll be back then," Marcus said, taking Abigail's arm. "Thank you."

"You're welcome." The receptionist's smile seemed meant

only for Marcus. Deep down, Abigail couldn't blame her. He was a very nice-looking man.

Once they were outside, Marcus turned to Abigail and asked, "Do you want to try the Palace?"

"Why don't we just make an appointment there for this afternoon or later this week? I think my chances of getting a good tour will be better if we set up a time instead of hoping for the manager to be free. Then we can head on back to the hotel. It will almost be time for lunch by then."

"I think that might be for the best, too." He led her to the next few bathhouses where they set up appointments for the next several days. Then they started back to the hotel. "I'll pick you up this afternoon around a quarter of three and tomorrow around ten again, if that is all right with you?"

"That will be fine. Oh, and thank your mother for the invitation on Saturday. I'm looking forward to seeing your parents again."

"You'd be welcome to call on them anytime, you know."

She did know. She'd felt it that first day when she'd met them. "I do. I just wouldn't want to interrupt their daily schedule."

"You needn't worry about that. If Mother were going out for the day, you'd be welcome to accompany her anywhere. You'll see as you get to know her."

His words made Abigail feel better. She had begun to feel a little awkward after seeing Marcus and the receptionist's reaction to him. After all, this was *his* town and a lot of these people were *his* friends. She was the stranger in town, and at the moment, she felt a little lonely.

It was nearing noon when they got back to the hotel and parted ways. She barely had time to freshen up before meeting Sally in the lobby. The other woman looked fresh as a daisy in a yellow and white dress, with a sheer overskirt in yellow draped to the side. Once they were seated at a table in front of one of the windows overlooking the street, Sally smiled at her. "I am so glad you were able to meet me for lunch. How are you liking Hot Springs?"

"Thank you for inviting me," Abigail said. "I like your town a lot—although all I've mostly seen are the bathhouses I'm checking out for my father. I'd like to see some of the shops, but I'll get to them."

"I'd love to go shopping with you anytime. I can show you where I like to shop."

"Wonderful! I'd love to do that."

"I also wanted to invite you to a dinner I'm giving a week from Friday evening, if you are free. You may bring an escort, of course."

"Why, thank you. I'd like that. Perhaps Mr. Wellington will come with me." Abigail didn't really want to get into the fact that the handsome man was only protecting her while she was here, but Sally probably had an idea, knowing the business he was in.

"That would be perfect. We always enjoy it when we can get Marcus to come to dinner, but it's not too often that we do."

Somehow that made Abigail feel better, and she wasn't sure why. She enjoyed the lunch with Sally, and they lingered over their dessert of coconut cake and coffee.

"I'd think it would be very lonely to travel alone," Sally said. "Don't you miss your friends?"

Truthfully, Abigail hadn't given her friends much thought. When she did, she could just imagine them discussing her broken engagement, and that wasn't something she wanted to think about.

"Actually, my life had become very busy, but I'm not sure any of it counted for much. I do miss my parents, though." More than she'd thought she would. Each day, she appreciated them a little more.

"I can imagine. I'm married, but I see my mother nearly every day. Are you planning on going home after you finish the business for your father?"

"No. I. . ." She liked Sally, and there was really no reason not to tell the truth. "I was planning on getting married. . . and it was called off. My fiancé is marrying someone else, and I just don't—"

"Oh, my dear. I am so sorry. I am just too nosy sometimes."

"You aren't nosy. It is all right. Actually, it feels good to tell someone about it. I just couldn't stay there."

"Well, I'm glad you are here. I would have wanted to do the very same thing," Sally said, endearing herself to Abigail.

Abigail found she could actually chuckle. "I just kept thinking that everyone in town would be talking about me behind my back, and I just couldn't face it. I don't think I'm a very brave person."

"I know I'm certainly not. Don't you worry. We'll find all kinds of things to keep you busy until you feel at home here. Why don't we go shopping soon? You can tell me how we compare to your hometown."

"Perhaps we can go on Monday?" Abigail had the rest of her week planned out, and she was sure Sally would want to spend Saturday with her husband; it would be nice to look forward to the next week, though.

"I'd like that. Just let me know what time is good for you."

"Let's plan on around ten, and then we can have lunch while we're out and keep shopping after or not."

"That sounds wonderful." Abigail was sure that since

Marcus knew Sally, they'd be able to shop alone. . .well, except for whatever agent he'd have watching them from a distance.

❧

Marcus felt all right about leaving Abigail with Sally. He had his man in the hotel and knew they'd be watched well. But he found himself thinking about her all the way back to his office. He could get quite used to being with Abigail Connors on a regular basis. He had to keep reminding himself that the only reason he was seeing so much of her was because of her father. Otherwise, she would most likely rather be left to herself.

He was glad she wasn't planning on leaving once her work for her father was done. Jacob had told him that she was coming for an extended stay, and he hoped she didn't get homesick and decide to return anytime soon. Not because he'd been hired by her father. Marcus would be watching after Abigail Connors even if Jacob hadn't asked him to.

Arriving at his office, he called his mother to let her know that Abigail had accepted her invitation.

"Good. Did you tell her that it was a party in her honor?"

"Well, no. I didn't."

"Marcus!"

"Mother, it will be fine. She'll be pleased. She said she was looking forward to seeing you and Father."

"I think you'd better tell her when you pick her up, then."

"I will." Marcus could hear his mother's sigh on the other end of the line.

"You be sure to. We'll see you later, then."

He heard the click on the end and had a feeling she was a little put out with him. He probably should have told Abigail it was a party, but he'd not thought it was that important at the time. He turned his attention to the mail he'd picked up earlier. Shuffling through the letters, he pulled out the one that interested him the most. The agent he'd sent to Eureka Springs to look into Abigail's background, other than what Jacob had told him, had some information for him.

Marcus scanned the letter quickly, but there wasn't really anything there he didn't already know—except that the man Abigail had been engaged to was her widowed brother-in-law. From all accounts, she'd been in love with him for a very long time. And now he was set to marry someone else.

Leaning back in his chair, Marcus could see how that would be a devastating blow one would want to run from. He folded the letter up and slipped it into the envelope. He couldn't understand it. Abigail was lovely. She seemed a little brittle at times, but after all she'd been through, that seemed understandable.

There wasn't much he could do about the hurt she'd suffered except pray for her, and he bowed his head and did just that.

"Dear Father, I don't know the facts on Abigail's hurt, and perhaps I'm not meant to. But You know I'm a have-to-know kind of person, and I'll try to find out so that I can understand her better. In the meantime, I just pray that You help her through the pain she must be feeling. Please help her to get over her broken engagement and be able to have the kind of life You want for her. Please help us to make her feel welcome here, and while You are at it, Lord, I have a feeling I'm beginning to care a little too much for her. Please help me not to lose my heart to her. She's not likely to return any feelings I might have for her. Not right now, anyway. Please just help me to help her and keep her safe while she's here. In Jesus' name. Amen."

ا،

Abigail was surprised at how much she enjoyed the evening at the Wellingtons' on Saturday night, considering how nervous she'd been when she found out that it was a party in her honor. Mrs. Wellington was so gracious and kind to do something like this.

She'd been introduced to Dr. O'Malley and his wife and to one of the pharmacists in town, a Mr. Primm, and his wife... Donna, Abigail thought her name was. She knew she'd never remember them all, but by the end of the evening, she had a feeling she'd met most of the people she might need to know if she stayed for very long. She'd already met the minister on Sunday, but tonight, besides a doctor and a pharmacist, she'd met a lawyer and a banker and their wives. They were all very nice.

She had a feeling she'd be receiving invitations for other dinners and outings very soon. Once the last guest left, she turned to her hostess. "Mrs. Wellington, I can't thank you enough for having me tonight. My mother will probably cry when I write her about your kindness."

Mrs. Wellington patted her on the shoulder. "I just want you to feel at home in our town, dear. And I hope you will feel you can drop in on us anytime."

"But—"

"And don't you worry about formality. You are always welcome in our home. Always. If we are not here, you feel free to come in and stay as long as you'd like. In fact, I think you should just stay with us instead of at the Arlington, although it is a very nice hotel."

"How sweet of you. But I can't impose that way."

"Abigail Connors." Mrs. Wellington sounded so much like her mother that Abigail found herself fighting tears. "You are my dear friends' daughter. That means you are family. You would not be imposing in any way, but I will try to understand your need to be on your own. Or at least accept it."

She smiled, and Abigail couldn't help but chuckle.

"But," Mrs. Wellington continued, "I will be very hurt if you don't visit often and keep in touch."

"I can't think of anything I'd rather do," Abigail answered honestly.

"Good. Now, how would you like to come with me to a meeting at church next week? We are trying to find ways to help those who come here to make use of the springs but can't afford to stay in the hotels."

Marcus had told her about the free bathhouses, but Abigail hadn't really thought about those who might not be able to afford to stay indefinitely. And even if she had, at one time she would have put it to the back of her mind. She was a bit surprised to hear herself answer, "Yes, I'd be glad to go with you."

"Good. It is at eleven o'clock on Wednesday. After the meeting, we'll have a nice lunch."

Abigail had never been very demonstrative, but she found herself hugging the older woman. "Thank you. Being around you makes me feel as if I have family here."

Mrs. Wellington hugged her back. "That's exactly the way we want you to feel. I wish your parents could come for a visit."

Abigail grinned. "If I stay long enough, perhaps they will."

"Then we shall strive to keep you here," Mr. Wellington said.

Abigail looked over the older man's shoulder at Marcus, and something about the look in his eyes made her heart turn over. When he smiled at her and showed his dimple, that same heart seemed to do a sort of flip and dive that left her feeling more than a little breathless.

The feeling didn't leave her until long after she and Marcus had said good night from opposite sides of her door.

The next day at church, Abigail tried to ignore the way her pulse raced as she sat beside Marcus. She had to admit that she didn't mind having him escort her wherever they went. It was obvious that he was well-thought-of and respected by those people she'd met when with him. And if anyone had heard of her broken engagement, she certainly didn't think they'd bring it up, knowing she was a friend of the Wellington family. All in all, she was very pleased her father had hired Marcus, and knowing her father as she did, he probably took the family friendship into consideration when he did so. That way, people wouldn't just naturally assume he'd been hired to protect her.

She stood up when the rest of the family did to sing a hymn and chastised herself for thinking about Marcus when she should be paying attention to the church service. . .and for all the times she'd let her mind wander back home when she was in church. She'd been attending all her life and could remember when she'd been baptized. But it suddenly hit her that somewhere along the way, she'd only been putting lip service to her Christianity. It was time for that to change.

seven

Abigail's mother had written to let her know that Nate and Meagan had set their wedding date for the third of September, and while she'd shed tears over it, Abigail also felt relief that she hadn't destroyed their chance for happiness. Over the next few weeks, Abigail began to feel at home in Hot Springs. She'd been invited to several more dinners and had gone shopping a few times with Sally. But the time she'd enjoyed most was the hours she spent with Marcus and his family. She loved going to church with them and then spending the rest of the day at their home. Usually, others were invited for Sunday dinner, and she was beginning to feel comfortable around them as well. It was hard to believe she'd been in Hot Springs for more than a month and that it was now September.

The days were still warm, but the leaves were beginning to change on the hardwoods on the mountain across from her hotel. She still had no desire to return home, and she'd begun to think she might want to stay in Hot Springs permanently.

On the weekdays when Abigail went with Mrs. Wellington to her meeting at church, Mr. Wellington picked her up at the hotel, and then she somehow ended up going back to their home for the afternoon and evening. Marcus would join them for dinner and take her back to the hotel. It had become something she really looked forward to. . .more and more each week.

Over the last few weeks, she'd been studying her Bible

in ways she couldn't remember doing back home, and this Sunday, she listened closely to the sermon John Martin preached. His subject was based on Philippians 3:13, on what Paul had said about *"forgetting those things which are behind, and reaching forth unto those things which are before."*

"Brethren, we must not dwell on our past mistakes but on what we are doing now and in the future. We must forgive ourselves as we have asked God to do and as He has done. We are His children, and each day, we must give ourselves over to doing God's will and not our own."

As he finished his sermon and they stood to sing the invitational hymn, Abigail felt as if the minister had spoken just to her and decided she wanted to think about this sermon and read her Bible more.

The final prayer was said, and she followed Marcus out into the aisle.

"Wasn't that a wonderful lesson?" his mother asked from just behind Abigail. "I think one of the hardest things for us to do is to learn to forgive ourselves. John gave me much to think about."

Abigail couldn't imagine that Mrs. Wellington had that problem, for she couldn't envision that the woman had ever sinned. Yet she knew that as humans, everyone did. Still, compared to all she'd done. . .yet. . . .

"You look very nice today," Marcus said, as he led her out to his buggy for the trip to his mother's.

"Thank you." Abigail could feel her cheeks heat up and wondered what it was about this man that could do that to her. She wasn't one to blush, but for some reason, she felt like a young schoolgirl when Marcus complimented her. She wanted to tell him how handsome he looked in his black suit, and she'd never found it hard to compliment a man until now. In fact, she'd found it quite easy. Had that been because she hadn't really meant it?

At the Wellington home, it felt quite natural to help Mrs. Wellington get Sunday dinner on the table. Like Abigail's mother, Mrs. Wellington tried to let her housekeeper take off on Sundays. Abigail was just now realizing that it was something she should have been doing with her own housekeeper all along.

She sighed. One more thing to feel guilty about. Then she remembered the sermon she'd just heard and had hope that she could put all of that behind her. For the first time, she truly believed that perhaps she could be forgiven her past mistakes—if she could become a different person than the one she'd been these last few years. It was something she needed to think more on—and she would as soon as she got back to the hotel.

&

Marcus watched Abigail from across his parents' dining table. She was laughing at something his father had said, and she'd never looked prettier to him. He couldn't put his finger on when it began to happen, but each time he was with Abigail, she seemed to be changing in small ways that were hard to discern. She seemed. . .somewhat softer—less brittle? It was as if that hard edge she'd seemed to have the day he met her was fading away, and she didn't seem so much on guard. Much as he would like to think that it was because she felt safe and secure knowing he and his men were watching over her, he had a feeling there was much more to it than that. Besides, she still seemed a bit wary around him at times. And sometimes she still looked so vulnerable he wanted to take her in his arms and tell her that he'd never let anything happen to her.

As if I can control those kinds of things. All I can do is see that she is protected to the best of my ability, but if her heart is still broken, there is nothing I can do about that.

The thought took him back a bit. Her broken engagement was none of his business; he knew that. Neither was her broken heart. Yet he wished he could do something—anything—to mend it so that she might look at him as someone besides the man her father had hired to watch over her.

"Marcus?" His mother broke into his thoughts, and he found that everyone was watching him. It appeared he'd missed some of the conversation while he was woolgathering.

"Yes, Mother?"

She paused with her fingers on her temple. "Well, I was going to ask you something, but as long as it took to get your attention, it appears I've forgotten what it was."

"I'm sorry, Mother." He couldn't help but chuckle along with her, though, when she laughed and shook her head.

"You looked as if you were miles away from here."

Marcus shook his head. "No. My thoughts were right here." On Abigail—where they seemed to stay these days.

❧

Once Abigail was back in her room at the hotel, her thoughts on the minister's sermon fought to be heard. She barely tasted her tea for all the realizations that filled her mind. Before she could forgive herself for the past and go on, she had to make sure she'd asked God for His forgiveness.

And how far back did she need to go to know she had? The Lord knew she wasn't to blame for Rose's death. But she'd had that moment of hope that because of her sister's death, Nate might learn to love her. Abigail could no longer deny that she had coveted her sister's husband. A moan from deep inside escaped, and Abigail slid to her knees. "Oh, please, dear

Lord, forgive me for wanting Nate for myself," she whispered. "And please forgive me for being so envious of Rose for all those years."

Abigail began to cry as she prayed. "Please. . .dear Lord. . . please forgive me. . .for drawing away from You." She wiped at the tears streaming down her face. "I didn't want to admit what You've known all along. I have been an awful person, Father. I tried to make Nate feel guilty so that he would marry me—and I almost succeeded. And now. . .I don't know if I ever really loved him or if I just wanted what was Rose's."

Tears flowed freely as she continued. "And if I hadn't been so hateful to Natalie that day, she wouldn't have fallen down the stairs. Thank You for letting her be all right now." Her sobs came from deep within her. "I'm so ashamed, Father. Please forgive me and help me to become the child You would have me be. I don't want to be the same Abigail who left Eureka Springs ever again. I don't want to be that selfish or self-absorbed. Please help me. And please, please let Natalie and Nate and everyone I've hurt forgive me. All of this, I ask in Jesus' name. Amen."

Abigail stayed there, her head on the settee, until her tears were spent. She felt a peace settle inside her that she hadn't felt in years, and she knew the Lord had forgiven her.

❧

Marcus looked through his mail, and his attention fell immediately on the envelope from Eureka Springs. It was thick, telling him that his agent had found out more about Abigail. For a moment, he wondered if he should have gone this route. After all, just because he could find out almost anything about anyone didn't mean he always should, he supposed.

Abigail had become more than just the daughter of Jacob

Connors to him. She was more than a family friend and certainly much more than his other clients. Marcus opened the envelope and pulled out the thick missive. He quickly scanned the pages and then read again, more slowly this time.

The Abigail Connors of Eureka Springs bore little semblance to the Abigail he'd come to know. He shook his head as he read. Apparently Abigail had, for the most part, lived a very selfish life in the last few years. She'd been mostly concerned with having a good time with her friends and convincing Nate Brooks to marry her. She'd nearly succeeded; but then her niece had an accident, and shortly afterward, her engagement was broken. Nate had recently wed another woman, a Meagan Snow. *Hmm, that still doesn't tell me who broke the engagement.*

Marcus got up from his desk and went to look out the window. From the sadness in Abigail's eyes when he first met her and the fact that her fiancé had married another woman, he had a feeling that Abigail hadn't wanted the engagement to end. But he had no real way of knowing. She'd changed some from when he first saw her, so it stood to reason that she wasn't the same person she'd been at one time. At least he hadn't seen any evidence of her being the kind of person this letter described her as being.

He picked it up and read it again. It seemed that before her sister died she hadn't been quite so concerned with her social life. It appeared there'd been a time when she hadn't been quite so self-absorbed. Perhaps the death of her sister. . .

He shook his head and dropped the letter on the desk. None of it really mattered. . .not now. The Abigail he'd come to care about didn't seem anything like the one his agent was describing now or in the last letter. And he had no way of knowing what was truth and what wasn't. All he could really go by was now. And be thankful that the Abigail he'd come to know was nothing like the old one. At least—he prayed not.

❧

Abigail felt like a new person. After confessing her sins to the Lord and asking for His forgiveness, she felt almost the same as she had the day she'd been baptized: brand-new and ready to begin a new life. She just had more of her own sins to try to forget and put into the past than she had back then. She knew the Lord had forgiven her. But she was finding it harder to forgive herself.

She'd written letters to both Nate and Meagan, asking for their forgiveness for trying to come between them when she knew they cared for each other. Abigail shivered just thinking back on all the ways she'd hurt them in her quest to get Nate to marry her. She couldn't blame them if they never forgave her. The letter she wrote to Natalie was even harder. She loved the child so much and had loved her since the day she was born.

Dear Sweet Natalie,

How do I tell you how much I love you and how sorry I am that I caused your fall by raising my voice and hurting your feelings? I understand why you ran out of the room that day, and I will blame myself forever for your fall. I pray that you have healed completely by now.

I do know that you think I caused your mama's fall that day of the fire, and I can see how you might. But nothing could be further from the truth. I can only tell you that my intention was only to get her to not go back upstairs when I grabbed her arm. I know it may be hard for you to believe that after the fall you had, but oh, my sweet, it is true. I only

*wanted her to come with us to safety. The Lord knows
that is true.*

*I love you and miss you with all my heart, dear Natalie.
I pray that someday you will forgive me for causing your
fall and love me once more. I will always
love you.*

*Love,
Aunt Abby*

Abigail felt better once she'd handed the letters to the desk clerk the next morning, but she didn't hold out a lot of hope that she'd be forgiven. She'd been so awful to everyone. And she was having a hard enough time forgiving herself—how could they do it?

She read Philippians 3:13 repeatedly each night, and she was trying to put her past behind her—but Satan always reminded her of her sins in one way or another.

Still, she was faithful to take her worries to the Lord, and she was happier than she'd been in years. She wondered if it showed when Marcus arrived to take her to the Wednesday ladies' meeting at church. His father had a meeting, so Marcus picked her up and then they went to pick up his mother.

He kept glancing over at her until she finally asked, "What's wrong? Do I have a smudge on my face?"

His dimple flashed in a grin, and he shook his head. "No. You just look very pretty today. Not that you don't look nice all the time. You do. You just look. . .happy."

So, he did notice. And he thought she looked pretty. She could feel the color steal up her cheeks at his compliment. "I am happy. Papa is pleased with the reports that I've sent him on the bathhouses, and I feel I can relax and enjoy my stay now. I really like going to these meetings with your mother."

"She enjoys them, too. She says you are all making progress on finding ways to house those who need the help."

Abigail nodded. "Well, I'm not doing much, but these ladies are very determined to help those who've been sent here for treatment by their doctors but can't afford the bathhouses or the hotels. Several of the churches have members who have an extra room and have volunteered to take in boarders for free. Others are talking to the town leaders about what the town can do."

"There is a need. No doubt about that. Perhaps they should talk to the park superintendent."

Abigail nodded. "I think that would be a good idea, too. We can mention it to your mother."

His mother was waiting for them when they got to his parents' home, and once Marcus stopped the buggy, Abigail moved to get down so that Mrs. Wellington could sit on the front seat beside her son.

"Don't you move, Abigail," Mrs. Wellington said. "There's no need for all that getting down and getting back up into the back and getting settled. You stay right where you are."

"But I don't mind—"

"I know you don't, dear." She was at the buggy, and Marcus was helping her into the backseat. "But I do."

Marcus looked at Abigail and smiled. "Stay put. She can be real stubborn when she wants to be."

His mother chuckled. "Yes, I can be. I've found I've had to be a time or two in my life from living with you and your father."

Marcus took his seat beside Abigail and grinned. "Now she's saying that Papa and I are hard to live with."

"I did not say that, Marcus Wellington!"

They bickered back and forth all the way to church, but Abigail knew them well enough to know it was all done in fun and with love. She relaxed and let them entertain her all the way there.

⁂

That evening, Abigail and Mrs. Wellington caught up Marcus and his father on the ideas the ladies were working on.

"We now have fifty families willing to house people who are in need," Mrs. Wellington said. "I've put our name on the list, too, Martin."

"I figured you would, dear," Mr. Wellington said.

"Well, since Marcus moved out and we can't convince Abigail to come stay with us, I wouldn't feel right if I hadn't."

Marcus laughed and turned to Abigail. "I knew she'd use us as an excuse. But don't you let it bother you any."

"No dear, don't. You both are saving me a ton of money this way," Mr. Wellington assured Abigail. "Lydia would be having me add a room to the house if she didn't have one or two free ones, wouldn't you, dear?"

Abigail had a feeling he was right, and she was even more assured when his wife agreed with him.

"Yes, I probably would have. Still, this won't be the answer forever. We have also decided to form a committee to go to the town leaders and also the reservation superintendent, as Abigail told me you suggested, Marcus. Surely, either the city or the United States government can help come up with a permanent solution."

"Yes, I agree they should. But these things take time, dear."

"I guess it's a good thing we are trying to begin the process, then," Mrs. Wellington said.

Mr. Wellington nodded in her direction. "It is, my dear.

I am certain that you ladies will make these leaders sit up and take notice that something needs to be done."

⁓

By the end of the evening, Marcus was convinced that the Abigail he'd come to care a great deal about was not the same Abigail whom his agent had reported on. Oh, she might be the same person physically, but otherwise, she was nothing like the woman described in the letters he'd received.

He'd just received a letter that day from her father, wondering if she seemed lonely and how she was doing and if she was adjusting to life in Hot Springs. Marcus felt he could honestly report that she seemed to be doing quite well. Over the last few weeks, he'd accompanied her to several dinners she'd been invited to, she'd insisted that she could go shopping with some of the lady friends she'd made, and he had let his agents make sure they were safe. He didn't want her to feel smothered. But as he came to care more for her, her safety was as important to him as it was to her father.

"Thank you for attending these meetings with Mother. It seems to mean a lot to her to have you with her."

"Oh, she'd do fine by herself. She feels quite strongly about doing something to help the sick who come here to get better. I'm sure my mother would do the same. Since I'm not a permanent resident, I don't feel I have much to say, but I'm glad to go and give your mother any support I can."

Her words had Marcus's heart beating hard against his chest. He didn't like the idea of her leaving. Was she planning on going back home soon? He couldn't bring himself to ask outright. "Have you given any thought to making Hot Springs your home?" Only as he waited for her answer did he realize how much it meant to him.

She leaned her head to one side and looked at him. "Not

really. But I'm not in any hurry to leave." She shrugged. "I do like it here a lot. Maybe it is something I should give some thought to."

Marcus allowed himself to relax. She wasn't going anywhere for now. He had some time. . .to what? Convince himself that he didn't care about her—or convince her to stay?

eight

As Abigail got ready to meet Mrs. Wellington for lunch on Friday, she was looking forward to spending time with the woman she'd come to think of as family. While she did miss her parents and Natalie, she had no desire to go back to Eureka Springs. She'd started a new life here, and she was beginning to like herself again. She had a feeling that if she returned to Eureka Springs, she'd revert to the old Abigail: selfish and self-absorbed. She couldn't—wouldn't—let that happen.

She watched in the mirror as Bea put her hair up. "I still can't do that half as well as you do, Bea."

"It just takes practice is all. And it is easier to put up someone else's hair because you can see the back much better."

"Well, I might make myself look presentable, but I always feel I look much better when you do it." And she did. But somehow it didn't matter quite as much as it had at one time. In Eureka Springs, her appearance seemed to take up way too much of her time. Now she usually forgot what she looked like as soon as she was ready to leave the room.

Bea helped her on with her dress, a purple print with a sheer overskirt that draped to the back.

"You look lovely. Are you meeting someone special?" Bea asked.

"I'm meeting Mrs. Wellington for lunch here. She reminds me so much of my mother it's almost like having her here. I do miss my parents. I wish they would come for a visit." It suddenly came to Abigail that while she wanted them to visit here, she still had no desire to return to Eureka Springs.

"She seems a very nice lady," Bea said. She'd met her once when she'd accompanied Abigail to the drugstore. "I'm sure you'll have a wonderful lunch."

"I'm sure we will." Abigail picked up her reticule and an envelope and turned to Bea with a smile. She handed her the envelope. "This is your pay for last week. Thank you again for helping me, Bea. I really do appreciate it."

"You are welcome. I'm grateful that you hired me. I'll pick up your dresses from the hotel laundry and bring them up before I leave."

"I'll see you later, then." Abigail headed downstairs to meet Mrs. Wellington, who would be arriving at any moment.

She recognized all of the agents whom Marcus had assigned to her now. . .at least she thought she did, but she'd been instructed not to speak to them unless she needed them. So she just glanced over and nodded an impersonal good day to the one currently on duty and then went to the front desk to check her mail. She had one letter from her mother, which she put in her bag to read later. She kept hoping she would hear from Nate and Meagan and Natalie, but she really didn't think she would. Before she could begin to dwell on the past again, she reminded herself that she'd asked for their forgiveness and that was what was important.

She turned to watch for Mrs. Wellington and found her entering on her son's arm. Abigail crossed the lobby and greeted her with a hug. "I am so glad you could make it today. I've been wanting to take you to lunch for weeks now."

"I've been looking forward to it, my dear."

"And I feel a bit left out," Marcus said. But Abigail could tell he was teasing from his tone.

"Oh dear. I'm sorry. You can join us if you'd like, Marcus," Abigail said with a smile.

He chuckled and shook his head. "No, thank you. I do have a meeting to go to. But thank you for the invitation. It makes me feel better. I'll be back to pick you up in a couple of hours, Mother."

"Your father said he can pick me up if you can't come back, dear. Just let him know."

"I'll be here, Mother," Marcus said, bending to kiss her on the cheek. "You and Abigail have a good lunch."

He waved good-bye to them, and Abigail led Mrs. Wellington to the hotel dining room where they were shown to a table looking out onto Central Avenue.

"Marcus has been telling me how good the food is here," Mrs. Wellington said as she looked over the menu.

"It's all excellent. I believe I'll have a salad and macaroni and cheese."

"That sounds quite good to me, too."

The waiter took their order, and the next hour and a half passed much too quickly as they enjoyed their lunch and conversation. Mrs. Wellington always entertained Abigail with stories of when she and Mr. Wellington and her parents were younger. It gave Abigail more insight into her family. By the time they finished their dessert of lemon pudding, Abigail felt she knew a side of her parents that she'd never been able to see.

When they left the dining room, they headed to the lobby to wait for Marcus to pick his mother up.

"Abigail! Abigail Connors!"

Abigail's heart sank when she recognized the voice calling out to her. She turned to find Jillian Burton, one of her best friends from Eureka Springs, standing at the hotel desk, evidently checking in.

"Jillian?"

"Why, it is you!" Rebecca Dobson said. Suddenly, Abigail found herself surrounded by half the group of people she'd spent most of her adult life with. There was Reginald Fitzgerald, Edward Mitchell, and Robert Ackerman. Abigail's heart seemed to stop beating, and for a moment, she thought she was trapped in her worst nightmare. But when Marcus came in to pick up his mother just then, she realized the nightmare was all too real.

❧

Marcus's heart stopped when he entered the hotel to find his mother and Abigail surrounded by people he'd never seen before. His agent was on his way to the group, but Marcus didn't wait for him as he strode into the middle and asked, "Abigail, do you know these people?"

The look in her eyes told him more than he was sure she wanted him to know. She knew them, but he wasn't sure she wanted to admit it.

"Of course she knows us!" a woman with curly red hair said rather indignantly. "We're her best friends!"

The color in Abigail's face seemed to drain, and for a moment, Marcus thought she was going to faint.

"It that right, Abigail?"

"I—yes, I know them." She turned in the circle and began to introduce them by name. Then she turned to Marcus and his mother. "Everyone, this is Mrs. Wellington and her son, Marcus. They are family friends."

All her friends from Eureka Springs smiled and were polite, but Marcus had a feeling they were sizing him up and wondering about the way he broke into their circle. Abigail hadn't introduced him as owning the Wellington Agency or explained that he was in charge of her safety, so he followed her lead and accepted that she considered him a family friend now.

"Please come sit with us while we wait for our rooms to be ready and our luggage to get here," Jillian said.

"I do need to get home, dear," Mrs. Wellington said. "You have a nice time visiting with your friends. Thank you so much for lunch."

"Oh, do you have to leave?" Abigail asked.

Marcus had a feeling that she didn't want to be left alone with these people, but his mother didn't seem to pick up on it. "I do. But I hope to get to know your friends while they are here."

Abigail turned to the group from home and smiled. "I'll be right back. I want to walk Mrs. Wellington out."

"Your friends seem quite nice, dear. Perhaps I can have them all to dinner one night?"

"That's sweet of you, but don't worry about it. I'm sure they have all kinds of plans," Abigail said as she walked with them to the door.

"I'll be back after I take Mother home, Abigail."

"You can stay here, dear. I can take a hack home."

"I'll get one for you, Mother." He turned back to Abigail. "I'll be right back."

Abigail nodded, but he couldn't tell if she wanted him to come back or stay away. It didn't much matter. He'd be back. He wasn't sure about those friends of hers. Not at all. It was a good thing Ross was on the job.

❧

Abigail pasted a smile on her face and went back to her friends. For some reason, it had never crossed her mind that they would show up in Hot Springs. They must have found out where she was and come to see how she was doing after her broken engagement. Now that she thought about it, it was a wonder they had taken until the middle of September to find her.

"It is so good to see you! You could have let us know where you were!" Jillian said when Abigail got back to the group.

"You didn't come just to see how I am?" Abigail knew these people. She'd never known them to take a trip to Hot Springs or anywhere else for that matter. Their lives were pretty wrapped up in the Eureka Springs social life, just as hers had been.

"Of course not. We didn't know you were here," Reginald said. "We've been hearing how much more advanced Hot Springs is and about the bathhouses here, the opera, the races."

"Eureka Springs has been pretty boring of late. . .especially with you gone," Robert said. He sounded just a little too smooth for Abigail.

"We wanted a change of scenery," Edward said.

"How are you doing, though?" Rebecca asked, letting Abigail know that she was most likely right about the reason for their visit.

"Very well." Abigail chose not to mention her broken engagement or Nate and Meagan's marriage. "Papa had some business he wanted me to attend to for him, and I've found that I like Hot Springs quite well."

"But you aren't going to stay here, are you?" Jillian asked. "You are coming home, aren't you?"

"I'm staying here awhile longer."

"Well, then. We must make it our goal to convince you to come back to Eureka Springs with us," Robert said. "But while we're here, I'm sure you can tell us the best places to go and all about the nightlife."

Nightlife and socializing. That was what they had on their minds. It was almost all she'd thought about at one time, too. But not now. Still, they were here, and they wouldn't leave her alone now that they knew where she was, too.

"There is a nice opera house here. I'm not sure what is playing now, but the desk clerk will know."

"Oh, I'll go check," Rebecca said.

"The hotel dining room is excellent, but there are other restaurants in town. Marcus will be able to tell you other places of interest when he returns."

"Marcus? The family friend?" Robert asked. He almost sounded jealous, but he certainly had no right to. Abigail had never given him any encouragement.

"Yes."

"My—he is quite handsome. Is he the reason you came here?" Jillian asked.

Abigail wanted to tell her it was none of her business, but instead she answered honestly, "No. But it is very nice to have family friends here."

Rebecca returned to tell them that there was a minstrel show playing at the opera house that evening, just as Marcus came striding through the hotel doors.

"You'll join us, won't you?" Jillian asked Abigail as Marcus walked up to the group.

"I don't know." Abigail hesitated. She didn't know whether to be relieved or worried at the realization that Marcus wasn't going to let her go anywhere, even with people she knew, without accompanying her. After all—he didn't know them.

"What don't you know?"

"Everyone wants to go to the minstrel show at the opera house this evening," Abigail explained to Marcus. Might as well invite him. Otherwise, everyone would wonder why he was with her. "Would you like to go with us?"

He looked into her eyes and said, "I can't think of anything I'd rather do."

Abigail's heart turned over, and for a moment, she forgot that he was just going along with her so that they didn't know he was really there just to protect her. *That* thought gave her heart a little twist in pain, and she was glad she didn't have to say anything as the group made plans to meet up in the lobby at seven.

❧

As Abigail waited for Marcus to pick her up, she couldn't remember when she'd been so nervous. On the one hand, she wanted him with her. If her friends thought she'd been moping around since her breakup with Nate, having Marcus as an escort should help put an end to that! On the other, she was afraid that her greatest fear would come true—that with her friends here, he would find out what kind of woman she used to be back home in Eureka Springs.

"Dear Lord, please don't let that happen. I don't want him to see me as I was but only as I am now." The knock at her door interrupted her whispered prayer, and she hurried to answer it.

Marcus stood looking quite handsome in his black suit and tucked white shirt with pearl studs and white cravat. She was glad she'd worn her favorite pink evening dress with white lace trim and a lace overskirt that draped to the side and cascaded midway down the skirt.

"You look very nice. Are you ready to meet your friends?"

"Thank you. I'm not sure about meeting my friends. I suppose I have no choice, though."

"You weren't expecting them, then?" Marcus crooked an arm for her to take, and they headed down the staircase.

"No! Of course not. I haven't corresponded with them since I left."

"Hmm."

"Yes. My thoughts exactly."

When Marcus chuckled, so did she, and by the time they reached the lobby, she was feeling a little better about the evening. Marcus wasn't the only one looking after her. The Lord had heard her prayer, and she would trust that things would go well.

They all had dinner in the hotel dining room together before going to the opera house, and her friends seemed to be on very good behavior. They had been known to get a little rowdy in the past, but perhaps the genteel atmosphere helped to subdue them. Abigail certainly hoped so.

Oddly enough, no one brought up Nate or his marriage to Meagan. Perhaps her friends cared more for her feelings than she'd given them credit for. More than likely, it was because they weren't sure they should in front of Marcus. Either way, Abigail still wasn't at all sure how she felt about them being in Hot Springs.

Marcus proved what a gracious person he was by talking to them all, asking about their trip, and generally showing an interest in them. No one suspected that he was a private investigator and was very good at putting people at ease. By the time they left for the opera house, Abigail could tell that they all liked him. Well, all except for Robert, who still seemed a bit jealous to Abigail.

The opera house was quite luxurious inside, and Abigail was a bit surprised that she hadn't been there before. But most of her evenings out had been in people's homes, and she'd come to enjoy that more than trying to find entertainment. Actually, she'd liked entertaining back at home, but most of her friends had preferred going out somewhere as opposed to hosting in their homes.

Several couples whom she'd met through Marcus and his parents were attending the event, and it was good to talk to them. Her friends seemed quite impressed that she knew so many people already.

"You seem to be fitting in here quite well," Robert said as they found their seats. "And most of who you know appears to be the town's elite."

Abigail felt her hackles rise as she took her seat between Robert and Marcus. "It wouldn't matter to me if they were or not. They are very nice people, and I like them a lot."

"My, you are touchy, Abigail. I didn't mean anything by my comment," Robert said.

But she knew Robert and what *was* important to him. Thankfully, the minstrel show started just then, and she didn't have to answer him.

The show was quite entertaining, and it felt good just to laugh after being so tensed up that afternoon. They were all still chuckling when they came out of the opera house.

"Well now, my good man," Reginald said. "Abigail has told us you would know the best places to go. Where do you suggest we go to get a cup of tea, coffee, or chocolate?"

"There aren't a lot of restaurants open this time of night. The Arlington serves until eleven, though. The Melrose Place is open, and there is a café around the corner that will be open for a while, yet."

"I think I'll just go back to the hotel tonight," Abigail said, knowing she'd have tea brought up soon.

"Me, too. All that traveling has made me very tired," Jillian said with a yawn.

"Well, if you are going back, so am I," Rebecca added.

"But the night is young," Robert said. "I'm not ready to retire."

"I'll see the ladies back to the hotel, if you gentlemen aren't ready to go yet," Marcus said.

"You're sure? Do you mind, Rebecca and Jillian?" Reginald asked. "I'm a bit too wound up to sleep just yet."

"It's all right—tonight. But don't make a habit of it," Jillian replied. "Go. I'm sure Mr. Wellington will see us safely back to the hotel."

That was all it took for the men to be on their way down the street, and Abigail wondered why she hadn't realized how. . .thoughtless they were before now. Had they always been that way? Abigail was certainly glad none of these men was her beau, as Reginald was Jillian's and Edward was Rebecca's. And although she'd let Robert escort her to a few functions in the past, she'd never considered him a beau. Even if she had, after this evening, he no longer would have been one.

Marcus procured a hack waiting outside the opera house and helped the ladies up, and then he took a seat beside Abigail. Jillian and Rebecca spent the ride wondering where the men might have gone and openly flirting with Marcus. Were their relationships that shallow?

By the time they got back to the hotel, Abigail was ready to go to her room, but Jillian and Rebecca had decided that they would like to go to the dining room.

"Won't you come, too, Abigail? We have so much to catch up on!"

Abigail shook her head. "Not tonight. I'm very tired."

"Well, you will spend some time with us tomorrow, won't you?"

"Yes, of course I will. I don't know how you two are still

going after the train trip here. I was exhausted."

"Well, you were most likely depressed, too," Rebecca said. "After all—"

The none-too-subtle nudge from Jillian stopped Rebecca's next sentence, much to Abigail's relief. There was no telling what she was about to say. But the next words out of the woman's mouth were no help, either.

"I'm sorry. I—"

"Rebecca! Come on. I think that the dining room may be closing very soon." Jillian took her friend's arm and pulled her away, waving back at Abigail and Marcus. "We'll see you tomorrow, Abigail. It's been nice meeting you, Mr. Wellington."

Abigail's sigh of relief was audible. "I'd forgotten how. . ." *Irritating* was the word that came to mind, but Abigail didn't want to seem childish or mean-spirited. She shook her head and looked up at Marcus as he escorted her up the stairs. "Thank you for escorting me tonight. Their showing up here took me somewhat by surprise."

"They didn't know you were here?"

Abigail shook her head and shrugged. "No. I. . .just needed a change, and I. . .haven't felt the need to let them know where I am. I'm not sure what that says about our friendship."

Marcus didn't comment as they reached her room and he checked things out for her. She was relieved that he didn't ask any questions, although she wasn't sure what he was thinking about her. Although, that did bother Abigail, she'd been honest, and she was glad about that.

He handed the key to her and looked into her eyes. "I enjoyed being with you tonight. Your friends might take some getting used to, but I'll accompany you anywhere you want to go with them—and I would even if I weren't keeping you safe."

For some reason, his words made her feel like crying, and she wasn't sure why.

nine

Marcus wasn't impressed with Abigail's friends. Not at all. He especially didn't like the way Robert Ackerman watched her. The man had come looking for her; Marcus was sure of it. He'd been in this business too long not to put a few things together. Most likely, Ackerman had found out where she was and then convinced his friends to come with him so it wouldn't look as though he'd sought her out. The other option was that one of the other friends found out where she was and convinced everyone else to make the trip, and Ackerman invited himself along. Either way, the man was here to pursue Abigail. There was no doubt in Marcus's mind about that. The only thing he wasn't totally sure about was how Abigail felt about it. Oh, he had a feeling she hadn't been very happy to see them all today, but he wasn't sure how she would feel about it in the coming days.

On Saturday, she asked him to accompany her out to dinner with the group and give them a tour of the town so that they would know where they wanted to go. Marcus would have thought that the men had an idea from being out and about the night before, but he was more than glad to be with Abigail for any reason.

During dinner in the hotel, Marcus was less impressed than ever by the people Abigail called friends. The young woman called Rebecca seemed to want to rub salt into Abigail's wounds over her broken engagement—the one Abigail still hadn't told him about.

"Nate and Natalie look quite happy these days," Rebecca said over dinner. "Life with Meagan must agree with them."

Marcus heard Abigail's sharp intake of breath, and even Jillian recognized the insult. "Rebecca!"

Rebecca immediately put her hand over her mouth and said, "I'm so sorry, Abigail. I didn't mean to bring up a sore subject." But the look in her eyes said anything but that she was sorry.

"I'm glad to hear that they are all happy," Abigail said.

There was a sincerity in her voice that Marcus hadn't heard from Rebecca. Abigail may have been hurt by the other woman's words, but she seemed to truly be happy for her ex-fiancé.

"That is kind of you, Abigail, after all the hurt you've been through."

"I'm doing fine, Jillian. Thank you." Her smile was genuine, and her friend seemed quite surprised. Then their attention turned to Marcus, and he could tell they were wondering what kind of relationship he and Abigail had. Well, there was no way he was going to tell them her father had hired him to look after her. No way at all.

"I'm so glad to hear that you aren't pining after Nate," Robert said, leaning toward Abigail. "You deserve someone much better than Nate Brooks."

Marcus didn't like the gleam in the other man's eyes. He was more certain than ever that Robert would be pursuing Abigail in earnest. He hoped she could see through him, but he wasn't sure. He'd seen her when she first arrived, and whatever had happened back in Eureka Springs had saddened her deeply. He could only hope that she wasn't so vulnerable as to still be flattered by Robert's attentions.

Deep down, he knew that was as much for his sake as hers.

The thought of her caring about another man wasn't one he wanted to dwell on. Not for even a minute.

❧

Abigail's heart had stopped when Rebecca brought up Nate and Meagan and her broken engagement. She'd quickly looked to see Marcus's reaction to the words, but his expression didn't tell her a thing. He was still unreadable as they returned after the ride around town. He excused himself to talk to Ross, who was on duty. "I'll be right back."

Abigail nodded and turned to the rest of the group. "Won't you all come to church with me in the morning?"

"What time is it?" Jillian asked.

"We'd need to leave here at nine."

"Nine! Oh my. I'm not sure I can make that, dear Abigail. That is a little early for me."

"For me, too," Rebecca said.

"Oh, don't count on us either." Edward took it on himself to answer for the three men.

"Well, should you change your mind, just meet me here in the lobby."

Jillian giggled and shook her head. "All right. But don't count on it."

Reginald and Edward escorted them up to their rooms, telling Robert that they would be back down shortly.

"Good night," Abigail called to them all before she went to the desk to check for mail, only to be a little disappointed that there was nothing from home.

"May I see you to your room, Abigail?" Robert sidled up to her and asked.

"No, thank you, Robert. You have a good evening." Abigail realized that at one time she might have been flattered by his attentions, but she didn't want Robert Ackerman to escort her anywhere now. She'd let him take her to the Crescent Grand Opening only because Nate had asked Meagan to go, but that had been out of sheer desperation. Now she felt bad that she'd used him that way, but there was just something about the man that she didn't trust. She was very relieved when Marcus came up to her and took hold of her elbow.

"I'll see Abigail to her room. Good night, Ackerman."

The other man didn't bother to answer—nodding, instead. But Abigail didn't like the look in his eyes. It gave her the shivers.

While she and Marcus climbed the stairs and he saw her to her room, she couldn't help but wonder what was going on in his mind. She wanted to address the fact that she'd been engaged, in case it was brought up again. Her friends might say they didn't know she was here, but she just couldn't believe them. And it was doubtful that Jillian or Rebecca would not bring up the subject of her broken engagement again.

But she didn't have to bring it up. Marcus did it for her. He handed her back her key after checking out everything in her room and looked down at her. "Your tea got here before you."

"Good. I can use a cup."

"I'm sorry your friends reminded you of a hurtful time."

"I assume you mean my broken engagement. . .as they were so eager to talk about."

"It can't be easy to have it brought up in the way they did. Are you sure they are your friends?"

Abigail couldn't help but chuckle. "I've been wondering the same thing. But it is all right. I am truly glad that Nate and Meagan are happy. They were meant for each other."

"Well, if you are all right with it. . .I just don't like to see others purposefully set out to hurt another."

Abigail caught her breath, for she couldn't deny that she'd done exactly that to Meagan on occasion. She sent up a silent *thank-You* that the Lord had forgiven her for it, and she still prayed that Meagan would. But how could she judge her friends for something she'd been all too guilty of in the not–so-distant past?

"I'm hoping it wasn't done purposefully."

"Well, they are your friends, and you know them better than I do," Marcus said. "I am glad for your sake that it didn't hurt as much as it seemed intended to do."

"Thank you, Marcus."

"Will you be attending church tomorrow?"

"Of course."

"Good. I'll pick you up at nine."

"See you then." Abigail backed into her room.

Before pulling the door shut, Marcus said, "Enjoy your tea. And lock the door."

She turned the key and heard him say, "Good night."

"Good night, Marcus." Abigail leaned against the door for a moment before crossing the room to pour her tea. Then she went to the window and pulled the drape slightly open, barely enough for her to see out. It had become a sort of game to watch for Marcus leaving the hotel at night. Tonight he was just coming out from under the portico—much sooner than usual. She supposed it was because he'd talked to his agent before seeing her to her room. She waited until he looked up toward her window and then turned to walk down the street.

She let the curtain down and took a sip of her tea. She'd come to depend on Marcus more with each passing day— and probably more than was good for her. But she was so glad that he was there with her the last few days, even knowing that he didn't approve of her old friends. She was finding that she didn't much approve of them either.

Her worry was that Marcus might judge her by the company she had once kept. And still was keeping by what he could see. Marcus was so unlike the men in her social circle, yet she wondered if she would have seen the difference a month or so ago. No. She wouldn't. And suddenly, she realized why. She was the one who'd changed. Not them. She wasn't the same Abigail she'd been when she left Eureka Springs. Part of her problem with her friends being there was that they reminded her of the woman she used to be, and that was not something she wanted to think about or go back to being. Never again.

She took another sip of tea and opened her Bible. It had become a nightly habit she didn't want to break. And tonight, she couldn't wait to get started. She'd just realized that the changes in her were because the Lord was working in her, and the joy she felt at that knowledge kept her reading late into the night.

❧

Marcus looked forward to driving Abigail to church. Other than when he saw her to her room the last two nights, there hadn't been a chance for any real conversation between just the two of them. And after the dinner with her friends the night before, his opinion of them hadn't changed from the first day. Well, perhaps it had gotten worse, but that was all. The two women could be very catty on occasion. Abigail might be trying to give them the benefit of the doubt, but on more than one occasion, he'd heard them tell Abigail how sorry they were about her broken engagement. But the look in their eyes told him they really weren't that sad, and they seemed a little disappointed that she seemed to be doing quite well. The men in the group seemed no different than a lot of the rich men who frequented Hot Springs, looking for a good time and a way to spend their money. It was all he could do to keep his mouth shut as he listened to some of the conversations going on around him.

Marcus always loved Sundays, but he was especially thankful for today, in that he would have Abigail to himself for the ride to church.

"Will your friends be coming to church later?" he asked as he helped Abigail into his buggy.

"No. They probably aren't even up yet. They never have attended church much."

"Oh, I see."

"I did ask them to come today, though."

She sounded a little defensive, and he quickly apologized. "I'm sorry, Abigail. I didn't mean to sound judgmental."

"It's all right. They were talking about going sightseeing last night. I let them know that I'd be having Sunday dinner with friends."

"I'm sure Mother would have been glad to have them over," Marcus said. And she would have; of that he was positive.

"Oh, I'm certain she would have invited them. But truthfully, I could use a break from their company for a little while."

It did his heart good to hear those words. "They do seem to be quite busy—"

"Searching." Abigail interrupted.

"What?"

"They are all searching."

"For what, do you think?"

"For ways to have a good time, for ways to entertain themselves, for happiness. All kinds of things. But they never seem satisfied."

Suddenly, he felt he had a little more understanding of why, in Eureka Springs, she might not have been the woman he'd come to know. If she was spending most of her time with friends like the ones he'd met, she wasn't keeping very good company as far as he was concerned. Not at all. It was a puzzle to him that she was even part of their social circle.

"How did you become friends with them?" As soon as the words left his mouth, Marcus wished he could take them back. The color seemed to drain from Abigail's face, and she sighed.

"Jillian and Rebecca are friends from my school days. I can't remember when we didn't do things together. Reginald and Edward became part of the group later, and Robert is fairly new to the group. I've only known him a few years."

"I'm sorry, Abigail. It really is none of my business. You are just so different from them. I just wondered."

"It's all right."

But it wasn't. She still looked agitated when they arrived at church. Marcus thought Abigail looked about ready to bolt out of the buggy without his help. By the time they reached the inside, though, she seemed calmer. He'd try to think before he asked another question about her friends. It was obvious to him that she wasn't really comfortable with them being here in Hot Springs—but his questioning had made her even more uncomfortable, and his personal curiosity was no excuse. None at all.

❧

Abigail felt herself relax as she listened to the lesson and spent the afternoon with the Wellingtons. It was good to be with people who felt like family and who she knew really cared about her.

"How is your visit with your friends going, Abigail?" Mrs.

Wellington asked over Sunday dinner.

"Fine. They are on the go a lot, though."

"I suppose they want to see what our town offers compared to what they are used to at home," Mr. Wellington suggested.

"Possibly," Abigail said, but she really thought they just came to find out how she was dealing with the heartache of knowing Nate had married Meagan. Thankfully, she was much better than they expected. For that matter, she was much better than even she thought she'd be by now.

"Abigail asked them to come to church, but they had some sightseeing they wanted to do," Marcus said.

"I'm sorry they didn't join you. I would have been glad for them to join us for Sunday dinner," Mrs. Wellington said.

Mrs. Wellington was one of the most gracious women Abigail had ever known, but she was more than a little relieved that her friends weren't with her. She wasn't sure what the Wellingtons would have thought of them. She didn't think they'd be any more impressed with them than Marcus was, and she didn't want them wondering about how they could be her friends as Marcus obviously had.

"There is a lot to see around here. Did they say where they wanted to go?" Mr. Wellington asked.

"They'd asked me about some places, and I suggested the Thousand Dripping Springs, Chalybeate Springs, and Mountain Valley Springs," Marcus said. "But the men seemed most interested in the McComb Racetrack."

Abigail was sure they were. And she wasn't going to let herself feel bad that she hadn't gone with them. Just because the old group from home was here didn't mean she had to entertain them or miss church and being with her new friends for them. After all, she hadn't asked them to come to Hot Springs. She would be nice to them, and she would spend some time with them. But she didn't have to revert back to the Abigail she'd once been. And with the Lord's help, she wouldn't.

By the time Marcus took her home, she was feeling more like the Abigail she wanted to be. She hoped that her friends were still out or that they'd retired to their rooms. It had been a good day, and she didn't want to run into them that evening. She was relieved that they weren't in the hotel lobby, and even though she would have liked to have spent more time with Marcus, Abigail didn't tarry downstairs for fear of running into them.

"I'm glad you were able to spend the day with us," Marcus said after he'd checked out her room. "My parents look forward to your company."

"It's become one of the highlights of my week," Abigail said. But she couldn't bring herself to tell him that seeing *him* was the highlight of each day for her.

"Mine, too." The look in Marcus's eyes had her heart skipping a beat. . .or two. He pushed away from the door frame. "Benson will be on duty tomorrow, but if you need me, have the desk clerk telephone me. They have the number. Otherwise, I'll be here around noon."

"Thank you, Marcus."

He grinned and grazed her cheek lightly with his knuckle. "You're welcome, Abigail. Good night."

"Good night," she whispered back.

She hurried to the window and watched until she saw him reach the street. But this time when he looked up, it was as if he knew she was watching. . .and he gave a little wave. *That man. His smile. . .his touch.* Abigail drew a sharp intake of breath. Why, she was. . . She turned quickly, stopping the thought she knew was there when a knock sounded on her door. She assumed it was her tea being delivered, but she was mistaken. She swallowed the moan that begged to escape at the sight of Jillian and Rebecca.

"My, you've been gone a long time," Jillian said, sweeping into the room.

"I spent the day with the Wellingtons."

"Oh? With Marcus or his parents?" Rebecca asked, taking a seat on the settee.

"With all of them."

"Then he really is a family friend?"

"Yes, he really is." She knew he was her father's friend, and she felt he was hers as well.

"Hmm. How close a family friend?"

"I don't see how that is any of your business, Jillian," Abigail said.

"Well, Robert has been wondering and wanted us to ask."

"It certainly isn't any of Robert's business."

"Abby, what is wrong with you?" Rebecca asked. "You've changed."

"And why would that be something wrong with me? Perhaps it's a change for the better." She couldn't help but smile at their expressions. It seemed she'd just given them a concept they couldn't understand.

"You really aren't that upset about Nate, are you?"

"I told you I was happy for him and Meagan."

"But. . .but. . .you never talked to us about it. You just up and left town."

"I am sorry I didn't see you before I left. And I was upset at first. But I've come to see that Nate and I were not meant for each other."

"But, Abigail, you loved him for so long." Rebecca looked at her in surprise. "How can you be over it so quickly?"

That gave Abigail pause for thought; she suddenly knew the answer, but she wasn't about to talk about it now. She just shook her head. "I really don't want to discuss it."

Abigail could tell Rebecca was frustrated that she wasn't getting an answer. Her huge sigh told it all. "I suppose we might as well go." Rebecca looked at Jillian. "You know how stubborn Abigail can be."

Oddly enough, her words didn't upset Abigail. Instead, she chuckled, garnering puzzled expressions from both women.

"You *have* changed," Jillian said. She leaned her head to the side and looked at Abigail. "And perhaps it is for the better after all." They exchanged a smile before Jillian motioned to Rebecca. "Come on. We aren't getting any more information out of Abigail tonight. We can talk tomorrow."

Abigail walked them to the door. "What did you all do today?"

"Just a lot of boring sightseeing," Rebecca said. "We did take a picnic from the hotel dining room, and that was nice. Other than that, it is about as boring here as it is at home on a Sunday."

"Maybe you should have come to church with me—that would have started your day off right."

Jillian looked at her closely. "Perhaps we should have. See you tomorrow. You'll meet us for lunch in the hotel?"

"All right. See you then." Her tea arrived just after they left, and Abigail was more than ready for a cup. It had been hard to avoid answering their questions when all she wanted was to be left alone with her thoughts. She hurried to get ready for bed, and then in her comfortable wrapper, she curled up on the settee with her tea and thought back over the evening and the answer to why she had gotten over Nate so quickly. There was only one answer: She had been more in love with the idea of loving Nate than she had been in love with him. She wasn't sure that what she'd felt for him was even love. . . not when Marcus Wellington could make her feel the way he did with just a smile, a look. . .or a touch.

ten

Robert Ackerman was waiting for Abigail when she came down to join the group for lunch the next day. "Everyone has already gone in and acquired us a table. I told them I'd wait for you."

He crooked his arm, and etiquette insisted that Abigail slip her hand to his forearm. But when he pulled her hand farther and put his other over it, she felt a chill pass down her spine. What was it about Robert that bothered her so? She glanced around quickly and found Ross watching from across the room. He nodded, letting her know he'd be there, and she relaxed somewhat. Marcus or one of his agents was never far away, and just knowing that gave her a feeling of security she'd never fully realized until now.

She and Robert were shown to the table where the others were waiting for them, and Abigail was relieved that the only two chairs saved were not next to each other. The girls had saved her a seat at one end of the table so they could talk to her, and the men had left Robert one at the other end. Breathing a sigh of relief, she greeted everyone warmly. "Good morning. . .or afternoon. Did you all have a good day yesterday?"

"We missed you," Robert said plaintively from the other end of the table. "I felt like a fifth wheel along with these four."

Abigail wanted to say he was the one who'd chosen to travel with the foursome. It wasn't her responsibility to keep him company. And then it dawned on her that it sounded as though he'd thought that once they got to Hot Springs, he wouldn't be the odd number in the group—and that must mean that he'd known she was there. She chose not to comment on that revelation, however. "It's a beautiful day today. What do you all have planned?"

"I wanted to do some shopping," Jillian said.

"We thought maybe we could do that and the men could... find something else to do," Rebecca said.

"Well now, that's not fair," Reginald said.

"Why not?" Rebecca asked. "We did what you all wanted yesterday. And we don't expect you to go shopping with us. Surely you can find something to do on your own."

Abigail couldn't help but giggle at all the sputtering from the men. She wondered if the long courtship Rebecca and Jillian each had with their beaus wasn't getting a bit old. After all, they'd been courting for more than a year now—in Rebecca's case, nearly two—and still no wedding dates had been set.

There was a bit of tension at the table as they ordered their lunch, and Abigail was more than ever convinced she didn't want to go back to Eureka Springs and run around with this crowd. Oh, she cared about them and would pray for them, but she no longer was interested in spending her days in boredom, waiting for the next exciting event to come along or someone to come up with a way to take one's mind off the fact that all they were really doing was searching.

"I wish you all had come to church with me yesterday."

Total silence fell for a few moments, and then Jillian spoke up, "I kind of wish we had, too."

The waiter brought their meals just then, and the subject was changed. Abigail wished she had the courage to ask one of the men to say a prayer, but from the way all except Jillian had looked at her when she'd mentioned church, she didn't think it would be well received. So, as she silently prayed for their meal, she asked the Lord to work in their hearts the way He'd worked in hers to show her that all that searching she'd been doing had really been for Him.

The conversation got back to the afternoon's activities, and the men decided to go visit one of the bathhouses. "You might want the desk clerk to see if you can get into a bathhouse. They stay pretty busy," Abigail said.

"What are you ladies going to do?" Reginald asked.

"We're going shopping," Jillian said.

"But you will join us at the opera house, won't you?" Robert asked.

"Oh yes, I forgot to tell you," Rebecca said, turning to Abigail. "The night clerk told us that Bailey's big production of *Uncle Tom's Cabin* is here this week until Saturday when Lillian Russell will be here starring in the title role of the comic opera *Patience*."

"I'll think about it. Perhaps I'll go."

Robert looked a bit perturbed that Abigail hadn't said for sure, but she wanted to talk to Marcus to make sure he could accompany her before she committed herself to going with them. She certainly didn't want Robert thinking he'd be escorting her.

She was very relieved when Marcus showed up just as they finished and entered the lobby. Abigail turned to Jillian and Rebecca. "I need to talk to Marcus a moment before we go shopping, all right?"

"Certainly. Why don't you see if he'd like to come with us tonight?" Jillian suggested. "The show starts at eight, and we'll meet for dinner here at six."

Abigail could have hugged the woman for suggesting that she do exactly what she intended to. But this way, she wouldn't have to answer questions about how she felt about him. At least she hoped not. Those were questions she wasn't quite sure she wanted to answer yet. "I might just do that."

"Jillian! Why did you do that?"

Abigail heard Robert's aggravated-sounding whisper to her friend, but she ignored it as she met up with Marcus, who'd been talking to Ross.

"Good afternoon," he said. "Did you have a good lunch?"

Abigail smiled but admitted truthfully, "I've had better. I'm going shopping with Jillian and Rebecca this afternoon, but they all want to go to the opera house tonight. Would you be available to escort me?"

"Of course I will. Ross will be watching out for you this afternoon, all right?"

"That will be fine."

He nodded and smiled. "Good. Have a good afternoon, and I'll see you this evening at. . .what time?"

"It starts at eight. But we're having dinner here at six. Can you join us then?"

"I'll be here."

Abigail's heart gave a little jump when he smiled and showed his dimple, and she found herself looking forward to the evening very much. "Good. I'll see you then."

⁂

Marcus watched as Abigail went back to her friends. He gave them all a wave and turned to Ross. "She's going shopping with the ladies. Just keep an eye out, okay?"

"Sure. Long as I don't have to carry their bags, I'm happy." Ross laughed. "I'll let them get out the door and then stay out of sight."

"Abigail knows you'll be there, but it's better to try not to be seen in case her friends get curious. I'm going to do a little checking on a few things, and I'll talk to you later."

Ross nodded and went back to his paper reading. Marcus figured his men were more aware of what was going on in the town and country than most of the people who visited Hot Springs, with all the newspaper reading they did.

Marcus headed back to his office with the express intent of looking into Robert Ackerman's past. Something about that man set him on edge, aside from the way he looked at Abigail. Perhaps it was just his personality, but if there was something there—if Abigail was somehow in danger—he needed to find out.

Her other friends had all checked out. They were just part of the rich and, to his mind, idle: always in search of something more, something better. Abigail had been right. They were searching for all the wrong things. He was so thankful that she realized that now, because he didn't think she had in Eureka Springs.

Marcus looked over the scheduling of his agents. He'd insisted that they all get telephones put in their homes in case he needed to get in touch with them in a hurry. It had helped immensely when he needed to change schedules. He looked over the agents he had hired. He picked up the receiver and turned the crank to get the operator.

"Miss Opal? Could you get me through to the Morrison house?"

"Certainly, Marcus. Hold on."

Marcus waited to be connected to Ben Morrison, one of his best agents, who'd just returned from an assignment in Little Rock.

"Ben," Marcus said when he answered. "I need you to go to Eureka Springs. I need you to check out someone for me."

"Marcus, I can't do it. Doc says the baby can come any minute.

I can't leave Melanie right now. I hope you understand."

"Of course I do. Don't worry about it. I hope everything goes well. Let me know when she has the baby."

"I will. Thanks, Marcus. I appreciate it."

"No problem. I'll get someone else." Although he didn't have a clue who—all his other full-time agents were on assignments. Luke came in just then from checking the mail and the telegraph office. Maybe it was time to give the young man another assignment. He'd been hinting that he thought he was ready to do some real investigating. Marcus couldn't really argue with that. He'd taught him about all he needed to know, and experience was the only thing he was lacking. Luke had been eager to learn all Marcus had taught him, and he was chomping at the bit to get away from his desk and into the field. It was time he put what he'd learned into practice.

"Luke, want to go back to Eureka Springs on assignment?"

His huge grin told Marcus all he needed to know. "Are you serious? Of course! What do you need me to do?"

"A little investigating."

If anything, the younger man's grin grew bigger as he nodded.

Marcus gave him what information he had on Robert Ackerman. "He may be clean. But I have a feeling there's more to him than he wants anyone to know about, so dig as deep as you can. If you have to go somewhere else to get more information, let me know."

"Yes, sir. I'll get on it. When do you want me to leave?"

"As soon as you can get packed and get on a train." Marcus opened the safe he kept in the office, pulled out some cash, and handed it to Luke. "This should see you until you get back, but if you do get low, telegraph me and I'll get some money to you."

"All right." Luke pulled out a pocket watch and looked

at it. "There's a train leaving this afternoon. I'll go pack and catch it."

"Good. Let me know when you get there and keep me updated. If you find out anything I need to know quickly, telegraph me. Otherwise, I'll be looking for your report by mail."

"Yes, sir. You'll be hearing from me as soon as I get there."

Marcus watched Luke walk out of his office and knew he'd put the right man in charge. . .even if he was the only one he had available.

❧

For the most part, Abigail did have a good time shopping with Jillian and Rebecca. Still, she was finding that they just weren't quite as humorous or fun as they'd once been, and she had a feeling they'd certainly say the same about her. She took them to the shops she'd enjoyed going to with Sally, but they weren't very impressed.

"Don't you have a dress shop like Meagan's here?" Rebecca asked.

Jillian nudged her, but it didn't seem to faze her. "She's making quite a name for herself in Eureka Springs. I've ordered several things for this fall, but she can't get to them yet because she's so busy."

"Rebecca! I'm sure that Abigail doesn't want to hear about how successful the woman who stole Nate from her is!"

Only then did Rebecca act as if she didn't know her words could hurt. "I'm sorry, Abigail. But you did say you are happy for them."

Abigail took a sip of her tea and wondered if Rebecca was testing her. She was glad she could answer honestly, "I am happy for them now. But at first, I wasn't. I was devastated when I left Eureka Springs. But I've come to realize that a lot of the hurt I've gone through in my life has been caused by my own actions and choices."

"What do you mean?" Jillian asked.

Abigail shrugged. She wasn't sure she could trust her deepest feelings with these two women she'd once confided in. "Let me just say that the Lord has shown me a few truths about myself in the last few months."

"What kind of truths?"

"I've been able to see how self-absorbed I have been. To see that I was just putting lip service to my Christianity, that I was always thinking about myself and what I was going to do next that would be entertaining." Although her words didn't paint a pretty picture, Abigail wanted them to know that she wasn't the same person who left their hometown.

"All I was concerned with was what I wanted." *And how I could make Nate fall in love with me when I wasn't really in love with him. I only thought I was.* That thought gave Abigail pause. That was exactly what she'd been doing. And how unhappy she would have been had all that happened? Two people who didn't really love each other married because of what she only thought she wanted! *Thank You, Lord, for making sure that didn't happen!*

"But Abigail, we've all done that. Just because you want to have a good time doesn't mean you are a bad person," Rebecca said.

"Of course not. But it is when it is all one is concerned with. When it takes away from enjoying doing for others, spending time in God's Word, and trying to live the life He wants me to live—"

"What has happened to you?" Rebecca said, looking at her as if she'd never seen her before. "You aren't the Abigail we knew."

"I'd say I'm sorry, Rebecca," Abigail said. "But that wouldn't be true. I like the person I'm becoming here in Hot Springs, and I don't want to go back to being the old Abigail."

"And who is the cause of all this change? Is it Marcus Wellington? I'll admit he's a very handsome man and would be a nice catch for any woman."

Rebecca just didn't understand, and Abigail doubted that she could make her. Although she agreed with everything Rebecca said about Marcus, her change wasn't because of him. She gave all credit to the Lord. "No. Marcus doesn't have anything to do with what's happening with me—except perhaps that I'm glad he didn't know me back in Eureka Springs. The Lord is the One who is changing me, and I'm ever so happy that He is."

Both ladies seemed at a loss for words, and Abigail had a feeling that she'd given them something to think about or that they didn't want to hear any more when Jillian said, "I guess we'd better get back to the hotel so that we can get ready for tonight."

"Yes, let's," Rebecca readily agreed.

Abigail was glad to go back, too. She almost dreaded the evening ahead and would have tried to bow out had it not been for the fact that Marcus would be with her. She'd told the truth that he wasn't the one who had anything to do with the change in her. . .but there was no denying that he had a lot to do with the fact that she was enjoying her stay in Hot Springs and had no desire to go home.

❧

Abigail looked lovely when Marcus came to pick her up. She was dressed in a bluish green dress that brought out the color of her eyes and made her skin look like velvet, and he was more than proud to escort her back downstairs to meet her friends. "You look quite beautiful this evening."

"Why, thank you, Marcus. You look very nice this evening, too."

"Thank you." He pulled her hand through his arm and looked into her eyes. He loved seeing the color creep up her neck onto her cheeks when he complimented her. It made her look even prettier.

Ackerman, Mitchell, and Fitzgerald were in the lobby when they got there, but it was Ackerman who hurried over and reached for Abigail's hand. He brought it to his lips, and Marcus's fingers itched with the urge to grab her hand out of his.

"You look lovely as always, dear Abigail," Ackerman said, looking deep into her eyes.

The man was a creep, and Marcus was relieved to see Abigail pull her hand away and put it behind her back.

"Thank you, Robert." She looked around the lobby. "Have Rebecca and Jillian come down yet?"

"Not yet, but they'd better hurry, or we are going to be late."

"We're coming," Jillian called from the staircase as she and Rebecca hurried down.

After a somewhat hurried dinner, they all went out to the tallyho the men had rented to take them to the opera. There was some juggling for position, with Ackerman obviously trying to sit by Abigail. The man succeeded, but as Marcus was on the other side of her, he didn't worry about it overly much. He had a feeling that Abigail didn't like the close proximity of the other man any better than he did. At least he certainly hoped not. As far as he was concerned, her friends couldn't leave Hot Springs soon enough. Especially Ackerman.

eleven

By the time Marcus took Abigail back to her room that night, she was very relieved to get away from the people she'd once considered her best friends.

"Are you all right?" Marcus asked. "You were awfully quiet tonight."

She shook her head. "Sometimes I don't feel I know my friends anymore. I mean. . ."

"You aren't anything like them, Abigail."

Oh but she had been, and one of her biggest fears was that Marcus would find out just how much like them she had been. "We just don't seem to have as much in common as we once did," she answered honestly. "And Robert—"

"Is he bothering you when I'm not around?"

"He just. . ." She shivered. "I don't like it when he is close to me."

"Don't worry about it. I will take care of him."

Abigail's heart flip-flopped against her chest at the look in his eyes. "I—thank you. I don't know how much longer they will be here, and I just don't want to have to keep warding off his advances."

"You won't have to. The next time I see him, I will make it perfectly clear he is to leave you alone." Marcus pushed a loose curl from her cheek, and his touch sent her pulse to racing. "Don't lose any sleep worrying about Robert."

"I won't." Abigail sounded a bit breathless to her own ears.

"Sleep well." He handed her the key, and a current of

electricity shot up her arm. "Lock the door."

She could only nod and do as she was told.

"Good night," Marcus said from the other side of the door.

"Good night."

Her tea arrived only minutes after she'd watched Marcus leave the hotel. She couldn't help but smile when she wondered what he'd do if she actually threw back the drapes and waved when he looked up. He'd probably grin that smile that made her heart beat double time and wave back.

She quickly got ready for bed and then poured herself a cup of tea. She sat down and took a sip and sighed. She wasn't sure how much longer she could spend time with the people she'd once considered her best friends without letting them know they no longer were. She had nothing in common with them now. Their constant pursuit of fun seemed childish, their constant gossiping about people they knew was irritating, yet. . .it hadn't been that long ago that she'd been just like them.

Had she really been as boring and self-absorbed as they were? Abigail's heart twisted in her chest at the truth that was there. Yes. She'd been all those things, too, and she certainly had no right to judge her old friends. Instead, she should be trying to help them, but how? Jillian was the only one who had seemed interested in the changes in her. Rebecca seemed disturbed by them. And Abigail wasn't even sure that the men had noticed, not that it mattered. The only man whose opinion mattered to her right now was Marcus Wellington.

Abigail sighed and took a sip of tea. The better she got to know him, the more certain she was that she was falling in love with him. But could he ever feel the same about her? Probably not if he ever found out what an awful person she'd been. Abigail slid to her knees and prayed, "Dear Lord, please don't let him find out. With Your help, I am no longer that woman, and I never want Marcus to know how selfish and horrid I was. In Jesus' name, I pray. Amen."

❧

Keeping in mind that she wanted to help her old friends see there was more to life than the search for excitement, over breakfast the next morning, Abigail asked Jillian and Rebecca to accompany her and Mrs. Wellington to the Wednesday meeting at church. Rebecca immediately turned down the offer, but Jillian took her up on it.

"I'd like to meet some of the people you think so highly of, and I noticed the free baths when we've been out and about. I think it's wonderful that some women are trying to help those who are coming for health reasons but can't afford to stay in the hotels."

"I'm not doing that much. But I love being around Mrs. Wellington and the other ladies who try to help others. You know, our mothers do the same thing in Eureka Springs. Wonder why we never got involved?"

"That is a good question, Abigail," Jillian said.

"Well, they are involved. They don't need us," Rebecca stated. Then she waved a hand as if that should be the end of the subject.

"There will always be a need to help others. Our parents won't always be here, Rebecca," Abigail said.

"Humph! What's wrong with you two? I wanted to go on a picnic today. The men have gone to look at some horses for sale, and I won't have anything to do."

"Come with us then."

But Rebecca dug in her heels. "No. I'll just visit one of the bathhouses and get a massage and then take a nap. See you both later."

"Don't mind her," Jillian said as they watched Rebecca flounce off. "I really want to come with you. I want to meet these people who've become your friends here. I miss you, Abigail, but you seem so happy here that I think maybe you should stay."

"I've been thinking of looking for a house. I do love it here."

"You aren't looking to become Mrs. Marcus Wellington?"

Abigail was suddenly at a loss for words. How could she answer that? It seemed Jillian had looked inside her heart and found her deepest wish. . .one she hadn't really let herself think about. "I—"

Mr. and Mrs. Wellington arrived just then to take them to church, and Abigail was saved from answering. *Thank You, Lord. I know the answer, but I don't want to put it into words right now.*

As always, Mrs. Wellington was gracious and very happy that Jillian was joining them. Jillian seemed to really like meeting everyone, and instead of going back to the Wellingtons for the rest of the day as Abigail usually did, the three women had lunch at a small café near Marcus's office.

"It is so nice to meet a friend of Abigail's," Mrs. Wellington said to Jillian. "We love having her here. You aren't going to try to talk her into going back to Eureka Springs, are you?"

"No, ma'am. I can't speak for the others, but I'm not. Abigail seems happier than I've ever seen her, and I think she should stay right here. Besides, if she's here, I'll be able to come and visit her when I need to get away."

Abigail had been holding her breath as Jillian spoke, hoping she wouldn't go into detail about how she'd changed. Now she realized that Jillian truly did care about her and what was best for her. She patted her friend's hand. "You'll be welcome anytime." It was nice to know that she meant it.

❧

Marcus was glad to know that Abigail didn't like Robert Ackerman's advances any more than he did. It would be his pleasure to put a stop to them. All he'd needed was to know that Abigail wanted them stopped as much as he did.

During the next week, he made sure that he interrupted each and every conversation Abigail and Robert had. It didn't matter if it was in the lobby of the Arlington or in the hotel dining room; Marcus was by her side at any sign of irritation on her part. Before long, he could tell from just a certain look or smile that she needed him. But the man was persistent; Marcus had to give him that. If Ackerman wasn't trying to get Abigail to sit by him, he was trying to get her to go for a walk to see the town at night. And no matter how many times Marcus heard Abigail tell him no, the man refused to be fazed.

Did these people have no life to go to back in Eureka Springs? They'd been in Hot Springs for nearly three weeks now. That they were wealthy was obvious from the way they spent money, but surely the men had businesses to return to. Marcus couldn't wait until the day he would hear them say good-bye. Why Abigail agreed to so many outings with them was beyond him, but at least she saved her Sundays for him and his family.

"I almost talked Jillian into coming today," Abigail said on their way to church that Sunday.

"Really?" Jillian bothered Marcus the least of any of Abigail's friends. She had manners and truly seemed to like being around Abigail.

"Yes. But she didn't make it down in time. I suppose she slept in again. Or Rebecca teased her so much that she decided not to come."

They'd arrived at church, and Marcus was helping her down from the buggy. "I know it would have been good for you to have her with you, but I have to admit I look forward to Sundays even more than usual."

"Why is that?"

He looked into her eyes and told her the truth. "Because it is the only day of the week I get to see you without them."

"Oh."

He wasn't sure if she was pleased at his answer or not, but he loved watching a warm flush of color deepen in her cheeks. As the day passed, he didn't think she was upset with his words, for she seemed to relax and enjoy herself as always with his family and the other church members his mother had invited for Sunday dinner.

The afternoon passed pleasantly as they played croquet and checkers and enjoyed lemonade and cookies. He hated to see it come to an end and hoped that he and Abigail wouldn't run into any of her friends when he took her back to the Arlington. At first, he thought he was going to get his wish, but before they were ten feet into the lobby, he heard Ackerman's voice as he came from across the room.

"Abigail! We've been waiting for you to get back. Come sit with us."

Marcus heard Abigail's soft moan as she turned to greet Ackerman. "You knew this is Sunday and I'd be gone all day."

Ackerman didn't even rise as Marcus and Abigail walked over to the group. "That doesn't mean we have to like it, my dear. After all, we did come all this way to see you."

"Oh? I thought you didn't know I was here."

"Yes, well, you are here, and so are we, and we missed you today."

"You all could have come with me." Abigail spread her

hands to include the whole group.

Marcus couldn't remember when he'd heard so much twittering as they made excuses.

"I overslept," Jillian said. "I meant to come."

"Well, we were out late, and I hadn't even cracked an eye open by ten o'clock this morning," Edward said.

Marcus was certainly glad they hadn't come along, but he knew he shouldn't feel that way. It was Sunday, after all, and it was hard to come away from one of the minister's sermons and not have much to think about. It always did him some good, so he couldn't see how it would do Abigail's friends any harm.

"You know I don't attend church often, Abigail." Robert's smile turned Marcus's stomach. He didn't know how much more of this man he could take.

"Now how would I know that, Robert?"

When Abigail's eyebrow went up, challenging the man to answer her, Marcus bit his lip to keep from laughing.

"We've known each other for a while now, Abigail," Robert said, sounding condescending to Marcus.

"We don't know each other that well. Anyway, it was a good lesson today."

"Yes, well, perhaps next Sunday, we'll go with you." That same tone. Marcus had to clench his fist to keep from using it on the man. *Lord, help me here. Please.*

"Yes, we should do that," Jillian added. "If we aren't gone by then."

"Are you talking about leaving?" Abigail asked.

"Well, we've been thinking it is time to get back home," Rebecca said.

"Yes, there are several events we don't want to miss," Reginald said. "You should come back with us."

"Oh yes, Abigail. Please, won't you do that?" Rebecca asked.

"No." Abigail smiled and shook her head. "I'm not ready to go back yet. I like it here."

Marcus breathed in a silent sigh of relief. Deep down, he'd been worried that Abigail might decide to go back with them.

"But your home is there, your family is there, and *we* are there," Robert said. "Surely you miss all of that."

"I do miss my family. But I've just been able to see you all. I don't want to go back right now."

Robert folded both arms together and sat back in his seat. Marcus had never seen a grown man pout before, but there was no other way to describe the look on Ackerman's face.

"Well, I will be glad if you decide to come back, but you seem very happy here, and I'm glad for you," Jillian said.

"I don't understand you at all," Rebecca said. "It's a nice town and all, but it's not home!"

Abigail chuckled. "I believe you are all getting homesick."

"Not quite yet," Reginald said. "But we must return at some point soon."

"Yes, soon," Rebecca said. "I don't have that many cool weather clothes with me, and the nights are getting chilly."

"You could always buy a new jacket," Jillian said.

"I could, but I don't want to. I'm having Meagan Brooks make one for me."

"Oh."

Silence descended on the group at the mention of the Brooks name, and Marcus found himself holding his breath, waiting to see what Abigail would say.

"I don't blame you. She's quite talented."

He could have laughed out loud at the look on Abigail's

friends' faces at her compliment for the woman who'd married her ex-fiancé. They just couldn't seem to believe she was being so gracious.

No one seemed to know what to say, and Abigail turned to him. "I think I'm ready to go up now. I'll see you all tomorrow."

Robert was immediately on his feet. "I can see Abigail to her room, Wellington. I'm on the floor above her, and I'm not going back out tonight. No need for you to bother yourself."

"Thank you but no, Ackerman. I will see Abigail to her room, and it is certainly not a bother. Good night, everyone." Marcus clasped Abigail's elbow and steered her toward the staircase.

"Thank you," Abigail whispered as he led her away from the group.

But they weren't left alone. Ackerman hurried up behind them and grabbed Abigail's free arm.

"Look, Wellington. Abigail and I have been friends a long time. I'd like to see her up."

Marcus threw his hand off Abigail's arm, gently pulled her hand through his arm, and looked Robert in the eye. His voice was soft but firm. "I will see that the lady gets to her room safely, Ackerman. I always do."

"Oh?"

"Yes."

"Should I take that to mean you are courting our Abigail?"

Marcus had about had it with Robert Ackerman, and it was time to set some limits. "I don't think that is any of your business, Ackerman, but you can take it to mean anything you want. Just be clear on this. Your advances to Abigail are unwelcome, and I will be the one you answer to should you make any more."

Robert backed off, his hands raised. "I understand. Completely."

"I'm not sure you do, but as long as you keep your hands to yourself and quit bothering Abigail, everything will be just fine."

Marcus hoped Abigail wasn't upset with his implication that they were courting. But if it kept Robert away from her, that was what mattered. He wasn't sure how she felt about it, as she was silent as they ascended the stairs and walked down the hall to her room.

❧

Abigail's heart was pounding so loud she was afraid Marcus might hear it. For a moment, she'd thought he and Robert might come to blows. But it looked as if she wouldn't have to worry about Robert bothering her anymore.

Marcus checked her room out as usual. When he came back to the hall and handed the key back to her, he surprised her by asking, "Are you upset with me?"

"Not at all. Why would I be upset with you? I think Robert finally got the message not to bother me anymore, and I can't thank you enough, Marcus. It was getting to the point that I dreaded seeing him at all. Truthfully, something about him frightens me a little. I don't know what it is, but—"

"Don't worry about him. I won't let him get near you again."

"Thank you," she whispered, and her pulse began to race at the look in his eyes as he bent his head.

"You are welcome." His head dipped toward her, and he lifted her chin to look into her eyes. Her eyes closed the moment his lips touched hers, and Abigail realized her heart had wanted him to do just that for weeks. She couldn't keep from responding, and he pulled her into his arms and deepened the kiss. She wasn't sure who ended it, but she had a feeling it would be a long time before she quit feeling the sweet touch of his lips on hers.

"I. . ." For the first time since she'd known him, Marcus seemed to be at a loss for words. He took a step back and then reached out and gently touched her lips. "I. . .I'd better go. Sleep well, and lock your door."

Abigail backed into the room, her eyes never leaving his. He pulled the door shut, and she inserted the key and turned it with trembling fingers.

"Good night, Abigail." His voice was deep and husky from the other side of the door. "Sleep well."

"Good night, Marcus." She didn't know how she was going to sleep at all after that kiss. Abigail sighed and leaned against the door, her hand over her heart. She was in love with Marcus Wellington. And whatever she felt for Nate Brooks was nothing compared to what she felt for the man who'd just claimed her heart with one kiss.

twelve

Marcus came back downstairs, hoping not to run into Abigail's friends again. But there they were, still chatting and laughing. He had to wonder if they were waiting until he came back down. Now that he thought of it, many times the men were just leaving the hotel when he came back from seeing Abigail to her room.

The idea that they were waiting to make sure that he did come back down quickly didn't sit well with him. How dare they think that he and Abigail—*I have no proof that is what they've been wondering. None at all.* Still, he had a feeling that was exactly what they'd been doing.

He took a moment to say good night to them and went to talk to Ross, who was on duty. He didn't even bother to keep his voice down, as the only people in the lobby were he, Ross, and Abigail's friends.

"Keep an eye out," he said to Ross. "If anyone bothers her, you know what to do."

Evidently, Ross had enjoyed witnessing the earlier exchange between Marcus and Robert. He grinned up at Marcus. "I certainly do."

"I'll be looking for your report tomorrow."

"You'll get it," Ross said.

When Marcus turned to leave, he nodded once more to Abigail's friends, and he couldn't miss the look of dislike on Robert's face. Well, too bad. Marcus didn't trust the man one bit, and he hoped Robert realized that he was having someone watch after Abigail.

The men might not be going out tonight—after all, it was Sunday—but he had tailed them one night after the ladies retired for the evening, just long enough to know that they spent most of their nights gambling at one of several clubs in town. That was one of the downsides of a growing resort town in which rich people thought they needed the same kind of entertainment they had back home. Some of those amusements would be better left back there, as far as Marcus was concerned.

He walked out of the hotel and looked up at Abigail's window. The light was still shining, and he wondered if she was having her tea and if she was thinking of the kiss they'd just shared. He knew he wasn't going to forget it anytime soon. He shouldn't have kissed her. . .because now that he knew how sweet her lips tasted, he'd be wanting to kiss her again. And again. Of that he had no doubt.

❧

"So, Marcus is afraid I'll make myself a pest, is he?" Robert asked Abigail first thing the next day as soon as she came downstairs.

Reginald and Edward began a conversation with each other, but Abigail had a feeling they were listening to every word as she asked, "What do you mean?"

"It appears he's hired someone to make sure I don't bother you." Robert nodded in the direction of Nelson, who'd come on duty that morning. "I'm sure he's been watching me. There was another here last night."

"There are men sitting in this lobby all the time, Robert. I believe your imagination has gotten away from you."

Jillian and Rebecca came down just then, and they all headed toward the dining room, with Robert taking the lead, obviously out of sorts.

"What is he upset about now?" Rebecca asked.

"He thinks Marcus is having him watched."

"Well, it wouldn't surprise me any if he is, after last night when Marcus told him he'd be seeing you to your room," Jillian whispered to her as they were being shown to their table. "Marcus doesn't want him around you."

Abigail's heart did a little flip. After that kiss she and Marcus had shared, she hoped Jillian was right.

"Then again, maybe he's going to watch Robert on his own." Jillian nodded in the direction of the hotel lobby.

"What?" Abigail turned to see Marcus enter the dining room with a smile. Her stomach felt like a hundred butterflies took flight as he crossed the room to their table. He wasn't looking at anyone but her.

"May I join you?"

"Of course."

He pulled up a chair beside Abigail, and Robert had no choice but to move his chair down. "Since your friends think they might be leaving soon, I decided to take off work the next few days so I can accompany you wherever you want to go with them."

"Why how nice of you, Wellington," Robert said with a sarcastic tone.

"It is very nice of you, Marcus. We'll enjoy your company," Jillian said.

"Thank you, Jillian."

The others in the party added their welcome to Marcus, but it was obvious that Robert especially wasn't pleased as he kept silent and gave his attention to the menu.

"Well, what shall we do?" Rebecca asked in a voice that sounded slightly whiny.

"What haven't you seen yet?"

"There can't be much more," Edward said. "I think we've been to every bathhouse in town, and we've been to the races—if you can call it that. We got to see some trial runs, but the season actually ended at the McComb Racetrack before we got here. We've been to the opera several times."

"We're going again on Friday evening," Reginald said.

"Well, what can we do today?" Rebecca asked. "I'm always up for shopping, but I think I've been to every shop in town."

"How about a picnic tomorrow?" Marcus suggested. "The weather is very pleasant in late September, and I know several places that you might not have been to yet."

"I like picnics," Abigail said. "We can have the hotel pack us one."

"Yes, we did that the first Sunday we were here," Jillian said. "It was very good."

"Let's do that, then," Rebecca said.

The waiter came to take their orders, and once he left the table, the subject changed back to what to do that day.

"Why don't we just take a ride around the countryside?" Abigail asked. "I haven't seen it all. The National Reservation is large; perhaps we can take a ride up Hot Springs Mountain and see the view of Hot Springs from there."

Several other ideas were thrown out, but Abigail found she didn't really care what they decided to do. Marcus would be with them all day, and that alone made anywhere they might go more special.

❧

On Friday afternoon, Marcus sat at his desk and rubbed the bridge of his nose as he pored over the detailed reports Luke Monroe had brought to him. He'd received a telegram from Luke on Wednesday evening, letting him know that his suspicions were on target: Robert Ackerman had a past, and it wasn't pretty. Luke had left Eureka Springs that same evening and was sitting across from him now.

"Good work, Luke."

The younger man beamed at the compliment. "Thank you, sir. I'm glad I could get some usable information for you."

Marcus looked at the paper in front of him and nodded. "I'd call this usable. First thing we have to do is talk to the chief of police. I put in a telephone call earlier." He glanced at the clock on the wall. "He's supposed to be here anytime. I didn't want to go there. I don't want Ackerman or any of his friends to see me go into the police station. We can't let Ackerman know that we're on to him."

"No, sir, that wouldn't be a good thing. I was afraid to put all the details in a telegram, but I worried all the way back that maybe I should have."

"I needed the proof you've brought me before I could do anything. I did ask the chief to see if he had anything on Ackerman, but nothing turned up."

"And of course that's because he's going by a different name now."

Marcus nodded. "You know, Luke, you did as good a job as any of my seasoned agents would have. Not everyone would have dug as deep as you did to come up with Ackerman's true identity. You've learned well."

"Does that mean you'll be using me in the field a little more often?"

"It definitely does." Marcus was proud of the young man. He had the makings of a great agent and had already proved himself.

"I'll be ready."

A knock on the door signaled the police chief's arrival, and

Marcus welcomed him into his office.

"Wellington, you don't ask for a meeting unless it's something worth my while. What have you got?"

"Have a seat, Chief." Marcus motioned to the chair beside Luke in front of his desk. "This young man has just come back from Eureka Springs after investigating a man who's here in Hot Springs. A Robert Ackerman, formerly known as John Baxter. Ever heard of him?"

"Actually, that name is familiar, but I don't know from where. Who is he?"

"A dangerous man." Marcus slid Luke's report and a WANTED poster over to the chief. "And someone you might be interested in putting behind bars. I certainly am."

Marcus had put an extra man to watching Abigail ever since he'd had the run-in with Ackerman on Sunday evening. Now he was more than glad he had, but he wouldn't rest until the police had him in custody. The chief scanned Luke's report. "I see he's been living off the wealth of others for quite a while. He's apparently married several rich young women and inherited their wealth after they all died of mysterious causes." He looked up from the paper. "All except for the last one. She was shot, and he's wanted for her murder. He's been wanted for murder for over two years?"

"Yes, sir," Luke answered.

"And this man is the Robert Ackerman you asked me to check out." The chief looked at Marcus. "The one who is staying at the Arlington?"

"He's one and the same."

"Is he there now?"

"Last I heard from my agent, he and several of his friends had gone out of the hotel." Thankfully, Abigail wasn't with them. His mother had invited Abigail and her lady friends over for tea, so at least he didn't have to worry about her being anywhere near Robert. "I do know where he will be this evening though."

"Well, let's come up with a plan. This man needs to be put behind bars, and the sooner the better. I don't want a murderer running around my town for one more day."

Marcus was pretty sure he wanted it even less than the chief did. "I've been thinking about that. . . ."

❧

Abigail opened the door to Jillian and Rebecca, who had come to Abigail's room to have Bea help them with their hair before going to the opera that evening. The young maid had been able to make a little extra money while they'd been there. While Abigail had wanted to learn to do some things on her own and had actually needed Bea less as time went on, Jillian and Rebecca had used her services in helping them get ready quite often since they'd arrived. Bea was happy to make the extra money, and they were happy they had someone to take care of them.

"I do hate to leave tomorrow," Jillian said as she waited for Bea to finish with Rebecca's hair. "Do you think you'll be home for Christmas? Surely you'll be home for that!"

"I don't know," Abigail said. She did miss her parents; she also wanted to see Natalie so badly, but there still had been no response from the child she loved as her own. Still, she didn't want to go back to Eureka Springs. She especially didn't want to go back if Natalie didn't want to see her. "Maybe my parents will come here. The Wellingtons would love to have them come for a visit, and that way I could stay here."

"But don't you ever want to come back?" Rebecca asked.

"I don't know. I do like it here very much."

"You like Marcus Wellington," Rebecca stated.

Abigail looked in the mirror and pinched her cheeks, trying to give an excuse for the color that rushed up her face. "Marcus is a family friend. I've told you that."

"Yes, you did say that. And I believe he is," Rebecca said. "But I think there is more to it. Robert does, too."

"Oh, Robert! He's just upset that I don't want to have anything to do with him."

"Mmm. But—"

"Rebecca, leave Abigail alone about all that. I wouldn't want Robert's attentions, either. And how she feels about Marcus is none of our business."

Dear Jillian. If there was one person she was going to miss, it would be she. She'd proven to truly be a friend. Abigail smiled at her now as Bea began to work on her hair. Perhaps it was time to change the subject. "Did you enjoy tea at Mrs. Wellington's?"

"I did," Jillian said. "Very much."

"So did I," Rebecca said. "She is a nice lady, and so were the others she'd invited to meet us. Too bad she didn't do that when we first got here. Most likely, we'd have been invited to their homes, too."

Have I always found something to complain about? Abigail wondered. It seemed Rebecca couldn't say anything nice about anyone without adding something negative. Surely she wasn't always that way. Abigail was more than relieved when the two women went back to their room to finish getting ready, and she sent Bea with them, happily. At least she'd finally learned how to dress herself!

❧

Marcus ran a finger along the starched collar of his shirt. He hadn't paid a bit of attention to the musical. All he'd been thinking about was keeping Abigail safe when the plan he and the chief had come up with went into action. When the curtain came down on the final act and the gaslights were turned up, he was relieved to see the agents he'd assigned to the opera house in position. They were there in case Ackerman became suspicious before they got outside. Marcus knew police officers were stationed just outside the door, waiting for him to give the signal.

He and Abigail were behind Ackerman, who was behind the others in the group. Marcus noticed Ackerman looking around as if he suspected something was up and held his breath as they went through the doors to the outside. Once they'd cleared the doorway, he stepped in front of Abigail to shield her in case there was trouble and called out, "Ackerman!"

When the man turned, four policemen immediately surrounded him and had him in cuffs. "What is this? What's going on! Wellington, you have something to do with this?"

The chief came up to him. "John Baxter, you are under arrest for the murder of Marie Baxter."

"What! My good man, I am Robert Ackerman. Just ask my friends here. They'll tell you!"

"His name is—," Reginald began.

"John Baxter," the chief interrupted. "He's only been going by Robert Ackerman for about two and a half years. How long have you known him?"

"About two years," Edward replied.

"And do you know where he came from?"

"Well. . .I. . ."

"He came from Kansas, where he shot and killed his last wife." The chief turned back to Robert. "Take him away, boys. Let's put him where he belongs."

"You had something to do with this, didn't you, Wellington?"

Robert yelled as they took him off.

Marcus didn't bother to answer. He breathed a sigh of relief that no one, especially Abigail, had been hurt. He turned to look at her. She and her friends couldn't seem to take it all in.

"I. . .can't believe it!" Rebecca shook her head. "I just can't."

"He murdered someone? How can that be?" Jillian asked.

"I—" Abigail shook her head. "I don't know what to say. He—I—"

"Let's all go to that little café around the corner and talk about it," Edward said. "I can't believe he's been part of our crowd and we never suspected that he could be a criminal."

"Could they have the wrong man?"

"I don't think so," Marcus said. "There is a lot of evidence against him."

"Is Robert right?" Reginald asked. "Did you have something to do with his arrest?"

"I told the chief I knew where he'd be tonight."

"Then you helped, didn't you?" Edward stated.

"And if you knew a murderer was right under your nose, you wouldn't have?"

"Why—I suppose I would."

"Let's get off the street and go talk," Rebecca said.

"I don't want to go anywhere but back to the hotel," Abigail said. She looked up at Marcus and asked, "Will you see me back to the hotel, please?"

"Of course."

"I'm much too wound up to sleep," Jillian said. "I—we need to decide if we are leaving tomorrow or if we should stay. . . ."

"I'll see Abigail back to the Arlington," Marcus said.

"Are you sure you won't come with us, Abigail?" Jillian asked. "We're just getting some coffee and dessert."

"No, thank you. I'm not up to it tonight," Abigail said. "Knock on my door and let me know what you decide, or if it's too late, I'll see you tomorrow."

As the others headed in one direction, Marcus and Abigail headed toward the hotel. But when he pulled her hand through his arm, she looked up at him and said, "I want to know it all, Marcus. Now."

thirteen

Marcus chuckled. He'd had a feeling Abigail would have some questions. He just prayed she wouldn't connect it all back to the fact that he'd been investigating her along with her friends. "What do you want to know?"

She shook her head and shrugged. "I'm not sure. I knew that I didn't like being around Robert. . .but that he was a murderer? I went to a ball with him in Eureka Springs once! It's just so hard to believe."

She shivered, and Marcus pulled her a little nearer. "Are you cold?"

"No. I'm just so appalled that he could do something like that. I had no idea. None of us did."

Marcus didn't doubt that for a moment. That she was truly stunned to find out about Robert was obvious, and he had to admit that he was relieved she had no prior knowledge of the man. But she was paler than he ever remembered seeing her. "Look, why don't we go into the dining room and have some tea to settle your nerves?"

She hesitated only a moment before she nodded. "Yes, that will be fine. A cup of tea sounds good. I just didn't want to discuss it all with the others."

Nor did he. Marcus asked for an alcove table so that they wouldn't be disturbed, and once the waiter had taken their order, he turned to Abigail. "I did have a hand in getting him arrested. I admit that I haven't liked him from the first. Just something about him put me on edge."

"I can understand that. But how did the police know about him?"

"I told them."

"How did you know about him?"

"I had him investigated. I sent an agent to find out what he could about him."

"Oh. . ."

"Abigail, when you've been in this business as long as I have, sometimes you just get a feeling about people."

"I suppose that makes sense."

The waiter returned with their tea, and Marcus waited until he'd poured them both a cup and left before continuing the conversation. "I'm sorry if my having him checked out bothers you. I just became worried about your safety when he was around, and I—"

"Oh, I'm not upset with you, Marcus. I. . .it's just hard to believe that someone I saw often socially is a murderer." She shivered again. "How—what exactly did he do?"

"He's made a career out of marrying rich young women. Three, to be exact. But they died from mysterious causes, and we think he poisoned them. All except for the last one. He shot her and ran."

"Oh. . ." Abigail put a hand to her chest. "He just shot her?"

"Yes. After making sure he cleaned out all of her accounts."

"I. . .I'm at a loss for words."

"I know. That kind of temper. I knew he'd been pursuing you, and I wasn't sure what he was capable of. From the first, something about him just. . .didn't set well with me." He didn't tell her that a lot of his dislike for the man was personal. He had never liked the way Robert looked at Abigail. . .not from that first day. He'd come to Hot Springs to find her. Marcus had no doubt of that now.

"Go on," Abigail prompted.

"Once my agent got back into town with the information, I contacted the police chief, and we came up with the plan for tonight. I didn't want one more day to pass with him in this hotel with you."

"Well, now that we know what kind of man he is, I certainly wouldn't want to have him here either." Abigail shivered. She sipped her tea and was silent for several minutes before continuing. "Thank you for. . .watching over me, Marcus. I know Papa asked you to, but I don't think I've ever told you I appreciate that instead of leaving it all to your agents, as you could have, you've done a major part of looking after me when I'm sure you had other things that needed your attention. Not only that, but you've put up with my friends when I know you haven't really wanted to. I. . .thank you."

Marcus reached across the table and took her free hand in his. "Abigail, you don't need to thank me. You are a fam—"

"Family friend. I know you say that. But when I got here, only my parents were the family friends. And I was a very spoiled, bitter woman. I'm sure that you wondered just what you'd gotten yourself into by telling my father you'd keep me safe."

"I think you were going through a rough time." Marcus hesitated and then admitted, "Your father told me you'd just gone through a broken engagement."

"Oh? What else did he tell you?"

He hurried to assure her that her father hadn't given him her life history. "That you needed to get away and that you'd be checking into some business for him."

He could see her relax and felt like a heel. What would she do if she knew he'd had her and the rest of her friends investigated? That he knew she wasn't the woman she'd been when she arrived in Hot Springs? How would she feel knowing that he knew a lot about her, but it didn't come from her father? Should he tell her now?

No. She'd been through enough just finding out a friend of hers was a criminal. He didn't need to stress her more right now. But he had to tell her before she began to put it all together. And he had to pray that she would forgive him when he did.

❧

As Marcus saw her to her room, Abigail felt totally safe and cared for. Something about being with this man made her feel special. That he'd had Robert investigated because he was concerned about her safety gave her hope that he might care about her as more than just an. . .assignment.

She'd canceled her nightly tea order on the way out of the dining room. She'd enjoyed sharing her tea with Marcus, although he only drank one cup to her two. It was a nice way to end the evening, and she hoped that once her friends went back to Eureka Springs, they might be able to end an evening like this more often. Of course it could be that once her friends left town, she'd see less of Marcus, too. That thought didn't set very well with her. Not at all.

Marcus took her room key and checked everything out for her as usual, and Abigail realized how much safer she felt knowing he always made sure her room was safe.

"Here you are." Marcus handed the key to her. "I hope you sleep well after all the commotion this evening."

"I think I will. Thank you for seeing me back safely."

"You're welcome." He leaned against the door frame. "Are you sure you are all right? You still look a little pale."

"I'm fine. It is just a shock to know that we've had a criminal in our midst. . .and that we befriended him."

"I'm sure it is."

"What will happen to him now?"

"I imagine he'll be taken back to Kansas to stand trial."

"Which is what he deserves."

"Yes, it is. Are you going to be all right?" Marcus tipped her chin to look into her eyes, and her heart remembered the last time he'd done that. It had ended with him kissing her. . .his head dipped toward her now, and her heart began to pump at double time. Surely he could hear it. She closed her eyes—

"Abigail! You *are* still up!" Jillian and Rebecca came rushing down the hall toward her room. "We were hoping you would be. You should have come with us!"

Marcus moaned and stood straight. "Your friends have the worst timing. . . ."

Her heart did a flip-flop at his words. She didn't like the interruption any better than he did.

"I felt a little better by the time we got back, and we had tea here," she said, explaining why she and Marcus were just now getting to her room.

"Maybe we should have come with you," Jillian said with a sly grin.

"You could have." Abigail raised an eyebrow at her friend. "I believe you were the ones who wanted to go elsewhere."

"You're right," Jillian conceded with a giggle.

"I'll let you ladies talk over the events of the evening and check in to see how you are in the morning."

"Good," Jillian said. "We can tell you good-bye then, Marcus."

"We've decided to leave on the afternoon train," Rebecca explained.

"Oh?" Abigail tried not to sound too happy, but she truly wouldn't be sorry to see them go.

"Yes. Reginald and Edward are ready to get back. Besides,

it would just seem. . .strange to stay now, with Robert in jail," Rebecca said.

"And they can't wait to get home and tell everyone about what happened," Jillian added.

"Oh, Jillian, you act like we are a bunch of gossips. You can stay here if you want." Rebecca flounced into Abigail's room.

Marcus backed away and gave them all a salute. "I'm sure you all have much to talk about. I believe I'll leave you to it. Good night." He smiled at Abigail. "I'll see you tomorrow."

"Good night." Abigail couldn't blame him for making a quick exit. She didn't want to be in the middle of this conversation. Jillian followed Rebecca into Abigail's room, and she had no choice but to join them.

"I just can't believe that Robert is a criminal!" Rebecca said, dropping down on the settee and throwing an arm over her forehead. "Surely they have the wrong man."

Have I always been that dramatic? Abigail wondered. "I don't think they do, Rebecca."

"How could we not have known he was that kind of man?" Jillian asked.

"Because, *that* kind of man goes to all kinds of lengths to make sure no one does know."

"I suppose so. But it's just so. . .disturbing."

"What all did Marcus know? Was he in on the arrest?"

"I believe the police chief wanted his assistance."

"And he put us all in danger to capture him? Surely they could have found a way to do it when Robert was alone."

"And when would that have been, Rebecca?" Abigail asked. She didn't like the implication that Marcus didn't care about their safety when she knew he did. "The police had people all over the place. Not to mention that Marcus was right with us. I'm sure we were in no danger—no more than we've been in all this time we've accepted him into our homes, anyway."

"Abigail is right," Jillian said.

"I suppose," Rebecca grudgingly admitted.

An hour later, Jillian and Rebecca finally went to their room. They'd discussed Robert's arrest from beginning to end at least three times and why none of them had seen what kind of man he really was. Abigail was weary from hearing it, but it was hard to turn her mind off as she got ready for bed. She was very relieved that Robert was no longer there to frighten her. The events of the evening left Abigail with mixed feelings. On one hand, she was appalled to find out about Robert. And she was disgusted that she'd had anything at all to do with him. Yet she was thankful that she wouldn't have to put up with any more of his advances. No wonder she'd been frightened of him. Maybe it was because her relationship with the Lord had strengthened and she was finally listening to the instincts He gave her. At least she hoped they were right because she was beginning to think that Marcus might actually care about her, too.

She knelt beside her bed and prayed, "Dear Lord, Thank You for this day. Thank You for letting Papa ask Marcus to protect me. I know I fought it at first, but I was wrong. He has done a wonderful job of keeping me safe. Thank You for letting him find out about Robert and for helping to capture him before he hurt anyone else. Please watch over Jillian, Rebecca, Reginald, and Edward on their way home. I pray that they let You work in their lives as You have in mine, Father. I believe Jillian wants You, too, and I pray that the others will, as well. Please watch over Marcus and his family, and thank You for bringing them into my life. If it be Your will, please let Marcus care about me the way I care about him. I love him so. In Jesus' name, I pray. Amen."

fourteen

When they all gathered in the Arlington dining room for lunch the next day before her friends left on the afternoon train, Abigail was more than a little pleased that Marcus joined them. Of course, the talk was still all about Robert.

"Edward and I went to see him this morning, and they've already taken him off to Kansas!" Reginald said.

"Why would you do that?" Abigail asked.

"You went to see him?" Rebecca asked. "Why? He's a—"

"I don't know." Edward sighed and shook his head. "We just felt we had to find out more, I suppose. To be truthful, I'm glad that we didn't see him. I have no idea what I would have said. I feel he played us all for fools."

"We were taken in, to be sure," Reginald said. "But I was surprised that he was gone already."

"I imagine the chief didn't want to chance his escape. No one likes the idea of a murderer on the loose," Marcus said.

"True, true," Reginald agreed. "How did you become involved, Wellington?"

Marcus shrugged. "I had a feeling about him from the first, and I sent an agent to find out what he could."

"It was that easy? Why hadn't he been found out before now?"

"I'd assume it was because no one else became suspicious enough to check into his background."

The waiter brought out their food just then, and the conversation stopped until he'd left.

"You sent an agent? What kind of agent? What exactly is it you do, Wellington?" Edward asked.

Suddenly, Abigail realized how truly self-centered her friends were. None of them had ever inquired about what Marcus did for a living. Not one. They must have thought he was one of the wealthy with time on his hands just like they were.

"I own Wellington Agency."

"And. . .it is what kind of agency?" Reginald asked.

"It is a detective/protective agency."

Reginald sat back, seemingly stunned. It was all Abigail could do not to laugh. How shallow they were. Had they but asked. . .

"You investigate people for a living?"

"Yes, if there is a need. My agency also protects clients. I assumed you knew, but that was probably egotistical on my part. Although my firm is getting more well-known all the time, it will never be the size of the Pinkerton Agency."

"I assumed you all knew, too. I'm sorry." Abigail looked at Marcus. "I should have told them."

"No need, really."

"Well, not unless we're the ones being investigated." Reginald laughed. "Of course, we aren't wanted for anything other than having a good time. It's good to know who to call on should we ever be in need of your services."

"Do you only have the one office here?" Rebecca asked.

"At present. But I'm getting ready to open one in Little Rock, and I'm thinking about opening up one in Eureka Springs, too."

"My, what interesting stories we have to tell back home," Edward said. "I'm assuming you've been protecting our Abigail while she's here, but why? She never needed protection at home."

"Yes, my firm is making sure Abigail stays safe while here. At home in Eureka Springs, she had her father and friends"—Marcus looked Edward in the eye—"and she knew almost everyone in town, but she'd never been to Hot Springs, and it was new to her. And, last but certainly not least, she is a family friend, after all. That is all the reason I'd need to watch over her."

"Yes, well, that's been quite obvious during our visit. Not something more the two of you want to tell us, is there?"

Abigail's heart stopped when her gaze met Marcus's. The look in his eyes was for her alone. She felt it deep inside.

"If there's anything we feel you need to know, Edward, we'll telegraph you," she said.

Rebecca laughed. "I think you've been properly put in your place, Edward! Let's change the subject. Talking about Robert gives me the shivers. When do you think you'll be coming home, Abigail? Surely you'll be there for the holiday season. I'm sure your parents are expecting you for Thanksgiving, and that's less than two months away."

"I'm not sure. I'll let you know when I do, though."

"Yes, we must keep in better contact now that we know where you are," Jillian said. "I will miss you so!"

The talk turned to their plans for the holidays and how many events were planned, but Abigail didn't feel left out. She had no desire to attend most of the events they talked about. For the present, she only wanted to be here. . . where the man she'd come to love sat next to her. He bent toward her now and whispered, "I know you are going to be lonesome without your friends for a while, at least. Would you have dinner with me tonight?"

"That would be very nice, Marcus. I'd love to." There was nothing she'd rather do.

No one was happier to see Abigail's friends off at the train station that afternoon than Marcus. And he was more than a little thankful that Abigail was standing beside him and not on that train, waving back at him with them. He couldn't bear the thought of her going back to Eureka Springs, and it was time to tell her how he felt. But when he did, he had to tell her that he'd investigated her. That he knew all about her life before she came to Hot Springs. . .and he just wasn't sure how she was going to take it all. *Dear Lord, please let me know when and how to tell her.*

"Thank you for seeing them off with me, Marcus," Abigail said as he saw her back to the hotel.

"You are welcome."

Abigail checked with the desk clerk and was pleased to be handed a packet of letters from home.

Marcus walked her to her room and, after checking everything out, he asked, "Will you be all right until I pick you up for dinner? Would you like to go see my mother?"

"I always love seeing your mother, but Jillian and Rebecca kept me up late last night. I think I'll just rest for a while and read my mail. I may need to answer some letters."

"All right. I didn't want you feeling too lonesome with everyone gone."

"I'm sure I'll feel a bit at loose ends for a few days. . . although to be truthful, I was ready for them to go. All except for Jillian—I do hate to see her leave. I found out that she is a true friend."

"I'm glad. But I know Mother and Father will be glad to see more of you, too."

"Spending Sundays at church and with your family have been the highlight of my week. I do wish my friends had come to hear some of John Martin's sermons while they were here. I think if Jillian had stayed a little longer, she would have. . .but the others. . ." She shook her head. "But it's not them who have changed. It's me."

Marcus knew she was right, but now wasn't the time to tell her. He could only pray that the Lord would show him when that was. "I'll be back to take you to dinner at seven, then."

"I'm looking forward to it."

Marcus's heart swelled at her words, and he knew he'd be counting the hours before he saw her again.

❧

Abigail undid the packet of letters and shuffled through them. There was one from her parents and. . .her heart turned over when she saw the name of the sender of the next letter. Nate had answered her letter! Had he forgiven her? She was afraid to open it for fear that he had not, but she had to know. Her fingers shook as she slit it open with her letter opener. She sat down at the writing desk and pulled out the letter:

Dear Abigail,

I thank you so much for your letter. Of course I forgive you—I know that you never meant me harm. My question is, will you forgive me? I should never have asked you to marry me knowing that I loved Meagan. It was wrong of me, and I am so very sorry for the pain I caused you. I know that you have always had Natalie's best interests at heart, and I know how much she means to you. Please know that Meagan and I have been explaining much to her. . .and I know that she loves you.

From your letter, I know that you will be glad to know that Meagan and I are very happy, and we wish that for you

*as well. We pray that you will find someone who loves you
in the way you deserve—for you have much love to give.
You will always be welcome in our home, and we hope that
you will return soon. Your mother and father miss you a
great deal.*

Thank you again for your letter.
Sincerely,
Nate

Abigail noticed a page behind the first. It was a letter from
Meagan. If anything, Abigail's fingers shook even more as
she began to read:

Dear Abigail,
   *Thank you for your letters to us all. Please rest assured that
you have been forgiven. As I've come to hear more about you
and your help with Natalie through the years, I understand
even more how much she means to you. Please know that you
are always welcome in our home, as Nate said in his letter.
You always will be. As Natalie's aunt, you are family. She
loves you and misses you a great deal. May God bless you and
keep you. We do pray that He will bring someone in your life
to make you as happy as we are.*

Sincerely,
Meg

Abigail found that she couldn't stem the tears of happiness
that flowed. It was several minutes before she could see well
enough to open the next letter. It had no name as the sender
on it, but it was postmarked Eureka Springs; she prayed that
it was the one she needed most of all. She opened it, and her
heart leaped at the realization that this one was indeed the

letter she'd truly been waiting for. She had to keep wiping at her eyes as she read the childish handwriting:

> *Dear Aunt Abby,*
>
> *I do forgive you. Please forgive me. I know it wasn't your fault that Mommy fell down the stairs. You were trying to save her, too. Like you saved me. I know that you love me, and you didn't cause me to fall down the stairs. I ran too fast and tripped. Please don't blame yourself. I love you, too. Please come home soon.*
>
> *Love always,*
> *Natalie*

Finally, Abigail knew she'd been forgiven. Her Natalie still loved her. Abigail gave in to the tears and let herself cry long healing sobs. *Thank You, Lord.*

❧

When Marcus arrived to take Abigail to dinner, she opened the door to him with the most beautiful smile he'd ever seen. She'd never looked lovelier. The dress she wore was different shades of purple, although he was sure it had some fancier name. Whatever it was called looked beautiful on her. Her skin glowed, and her eyes were shining in a way he'd never seen before. Maybe her friends should have left a week or so ago, if their going had this kind of effect on Abigail.

"You look beautiful tonight," he said.

"Thank you." She gathered her bag, and after making sure the door was locked, they headed downstairs. Marcus had made reservations for them and asked for an out-of-the-way table that overlooked the street. Abigail liked looking out at the streetlights, and he wanted somewhere fairly quiet. Last night had been the only evening in weeks that he'd had her to himself for any length of time, and they'd spent that talking about Robert Ackerman. Marcus wasn't going to miss her friends at all.

They were shown to a corner table that had a view of the street yet was more private than some of the others. He held Abigail's chair for her and then sat down across from her. The waiter placed menus in front of them and then left them alone.

"Were you able to rest this afternoon?" She looked. . .more refreshed and alive than he could ever remember.

"I didn't take a nap, but I can't remember when I've had a better afternoon. The letters I received gave me joy."

Marcus wanted to ask about them but didn't feel he had the right to yet. And once he told Abigail about looking into her past, as he knew he must, he might never have that right.

&

Abigail had never experienced a more perfect night. She didn't know if it was because of the forgiveness she'd received from her letters or from Marcus sitting across from her. She had a feeling it was a combination of both. From the time Marcus had picked her up, she'd felt more special than she ever had in her life. The look in his eyes told her that he found her attractive, that he was happy being with her, too. She was beginning to believe that she could put her past behind her and look to a future.

She'd let him order for her, and they had the same meal they'd enjoyed on the first night they'd eaten together. Only this time, it felt special—as if it were their meal, their evening.

"I have to tell you that I wasn't real sorry to see your friends take off." His dimple flashed as he grinned at her.

She couldn't help but laugh. "They can be quite—"

"Irritating to be around—I'm sorry, Abigail. I shouldn't have said that. I'm sure they aren't irritating to you, but it got a little tiring not being able to. . . " Marcus stopped and shook his head. "Never mind. I guess I just resented the fact that I rarely saw you without them."

At his admission, Abigail's heart turned to mush. He'd missed being with her. . .just as she'd missed him. Hope soared inside that what she was feeling—what she hoped *he* was feeling—was real and not just a dream.

fifteen

Marcus sat beside Abigail in church the next day, disgusted with himself. He hadn't been able to bring himself to tell Abigail about looking into her past the night before. It had been such a perfect evening—one he'd remember forever. He'd told himself that he'd waited this long; surely he could wait a little longer.

The sermon was one he needed to convince him he had to tell Abigail everything. Minister Martin preached on secrets and truth. The verse that seemed to speak to Marcus's heart was Luke 8:17. *"For nothing is secret, that shall not be made manifest; neither any thing hid, that shall not be known and come abroad."* He could not put off letting Abigail know he'd had her life looked into any longer. She would eventually find out. He knew that. But even more, he didn't want to keep a secret from Abigail ever again, and he wanted her to know she could tell him anything.

He would tell her tonight when he took her back to the hotel. It was time. But in the meantime, he was going to enjoy the afternoon with her at his parents' home. He loved Sundays. It was the only day of the week that he was able to spend the whole day with Abigail.

Now he watched her from across the table and knew without a doubt that this was the woman he wanted to marry. And he had a feeling his parents wanted the same thing for him.

"Are you going to miss your friends, dear?" his mother asked Abigail.

"Not terribly. I will miss Jillian the most. But the rest of them are easier to take in small doses, I've found. I'm sure they feel the same about me after this visit."

"I don't know how anyone could tire of being in your company, Abigail," Marcus's father said. "We enjoy you immensely."

"Well, I think I've changed from the friend they counted on me to be. I. . .have changed in the last few months, and although I like the changes, I'm not certain that they all do."

"We all grow at different paces. . .in all kinds of ways."

"It was time I did some changing," Abigail said. "And I believe I had to leave home to do it. I'm not sure that I ever would have if I'd stayed in Eureka Springs."

"Well, I know you will want to go back to see your parents, but we'd love to see you make your home here."

"All of us would like that," Marcus said, his gaze catching Abigail's and holding it. He watched the delicate color flush her cheeks and hoped that what he thought she might feel toward him was right.

The afternoon went by much too fast, as the days were getting shorter, and after sharing a light supper with his parents, they decided it was time to head back to the hotel. It had turned cooler out, and his mother insisted that Abigail wear one of her light jackets on the way back.

"Are you warm enough?" Marcus asked as they headed back to the hotel.

"Yes, thank you. It's a lovely evening, isn't it? I love this time of year." The streetlights were being lit as he drove down Central Avenue, and lights were being lit in houses up the hillside.

"Would you like to take a drive, or are you too tired?"

"I'd love to take a ride."

Marcus steered the buggy past the Arlington, taking it to

the right at the Central Avenue and Fountain Street split, then following Park Avenue past the Waverly Hotel and the Hays House, which was undergoing renovations. He turned and made the circle back.

"Oh, it's lovely at night from up here!"

"Yes, it is." *But nowhere as beautiful as you are.* Her eyes were sparkling as bright as the stars she was looking at. Marcus wanted to tell her his thoughts, but he had to be truthful with her. The longer he put it off, the more he feared she'd never forgive him. When they arrived back at the Arlington, he wanted to delay the moment of truth as long as he could and thought about asking if she wanted to go to the dining room for a cup of tea. Instead, he walked her to her room as always, checking it out and then coming to stand in the hall beside her. "If you aren't too tired, I'd like to talk to you about something."

"No. I'm not tired. What do you want to talk about?" Abigail asked.

Upholstered benches had been placed here and there in the wide hallway, and he motioned her to one. "Would you like to sit?"

"Do I need to?"

"I'm not sure how you are going to take what I'm about to say."

"Let's sit, then."

Marcus led her to the bench and sat down beside her. "Abigail, there is something I should have already told you."

"What? What is wrong? Is there more about Robert?"

"No. No, this has nothing to do with him. It has to do with you."

"With me?" She looked at him with a question in her expression. "What is it?"

Marcus found he couldn't sit still. He got up and paced in front of the bench. "I'm afraid I'm not very proud of myself."

"What have you done?"

"I'm not sure it's what I have done as much as what I have not done."

"Marcus! What are you talking about? Tell me."

He dropped down on the bench beside her and took one of her hands in his. "Robert isn't the only one I had checked out."

"The rest of my friends—you investigated them, too?"

"I did. And not only them—"

Abigail jumped to her feet, pulling her hand from his. "You checked into my background, too?"

He hesitated. Oh, how he wanted to deny it. But he couldn't. He looked her in the eye. "I did. I wanted to know more about you so that—"

"No! I don't want to hear any more. You know all about me. You know how—"

"Abigail, there was no—"

"No. I can't believe you didn't tell me—"Abigail rushed into her room and slammed the door.

"Abigail. Please, listen to what I have to say."

"Go away, Marcus. Just go away."

He thought he heard her begin to cry, but he couldn't stand outside her room and pound on the door until she opened it. He couldn't compromise her reputation that way. "I'm sorry, Abigail."

Silence answered him from the other side of the door.

❧

Abigail let the tears flow. All her hopes of a future with Marcus were gone. Had never really been—not after he found out what kind of woman she'd been back home. She readied herself for bed without even realizing she did, her thoughts on all that Marcus must have learned about her.

The maid arrived with her nightly pot of tea, and Abigail motioned for her to set it on the table.

"Are you all right, Miss Connors? Can I get you anything?"

"No. Please. Just. . .thank you. . .but just go. I'm all right."

"Yes, ma'am."

Abigail poured a cup of tea but found she couldn't drink it. She sat but found she couldn't sit still. She paced her room. Back and forth in front of the fireplace. What was she to do now? Her heart twisted so tightly she thought it would surely break. She'd known Marcus was protecting her because her father asked him to. . .but she'd begun to feel that he had come to care for her just as she did him. It no longer mattered that he'd started out looking after her because of her father.

But now. . .to find that he'd had her investigated, asked questions about her, found out what a horrid, selfish person she was. She shuddered. All her dreaming about a future with him had been just that. A dream. There was no way a man like him would fall in love with a woman like she'd been. How could he see her as the woman she'd become now after all he'd found out? And how could she stay in Hot Springs knowing all that he knew?

After a sleepless night, Abigail got out of bed as soon as it was light outside. At some time in the middle of the long night, she'd come to the conclusion that it might be time to go back home. She'd only thought it would be hard to stay in Eureka Springs and watch Nate and Meagan start a new life. To stay here and see the disappointment Marcus must feel after just learning about how selfish, conniving, and hateful she'd been. . .

No. She couldn't do it. She had to leave. Much as she loved Hot Springs, she couldn't stay under those circumstances. Couldn't watch what might have been caring for her turn to disgust. She hurriedly dressed and then pulled the cord to alert the desk that she wanted service. Then she began packing. She knew there was a midmorning train to Eureka Springs because her friends had debated taking it or the later one. She wanted to be on the earliest one she could get.

When the maid came up, she was pleased to see it was Bea, but she was sad, too. She'd come to like the young woman. She had written a letter of recommendation to the hotel manager, suggesting that he put Bea on full time when an opening came up. And she'd left a note with a large tip for her. That was the least she could do.

"What is it, Miss Connors? You are up awfully early!"

"Yes, I've decided to go home. I need to have the clerk procure me a ticket on the morning train to Eureka Springs. Would you let him know? And then can you come back and help me pack?"

"Of course. But oh, I do hate to see you go! I thought that maybe you'd be marrying and staying in Hot Springs."

Abigail turned quickly to keep Bea from seeing her tears. That was exactly what she'd been hoping for, too. "I guess that isn't to be."

❧

Marcus hadn't slept at all. He'd tossed and turned until he finally flung the covers off and got up to pace his room. But that did no good, either. Finally, just before dawn, he'd gotten dressed and gone for a walk, praying for an answer to his distress. Surely Abigail would hear him out today. Last night, she'd never let him tell her how he felt about her, never let him explain that none of her past mattered. Of course, he really couldn't blame her. For the first time, he realized how invasive his profession could be and how he wouldn't like it if someone had been poking into his past for no reason other than that they just wanted to know.

It gave him pause. He knew he provided a needed service. Had he not had Ackerman investigated, the man could still be free to hurt someone else. And what he had found out about Abigail's other friends was only because of wanting to know more about her. But he shouldn't have looked into her past. Her father had given him all the information he needed. Yes, he wanted to know why she was so sad, and though he'd wanted to help her, he should have asked her. . .not gone about it the way he had.

Before he got to the Arlington, he knew something was wrong. Nelson was pacing back and forth outside the hotel.

"I had the desk clerk ring through to the office for me and had Luke see if you were in your apartment. Ross followed Miss Connors to the train station. She left a half hour ago. She had the clerk reserve a ticket to Eureka Springs for her. I have a hack hired. Let's go!"

Both men hurried to the hack, and Marcus didn't even ask Nelson why he thought he should be going, too. At the moment, all he could think of was stopping Abigail from taking that train. "To the train station as fast as you can get there!" he told the driver.

Both passengers were flung to the back of their seats as the driver proceeded to do just as Marcus had asked. When the driver reined the horse in at the station, Marcus left payment to Nelson. He'd settle up with him later. He ran into the building and scanned the crowd of people either just coming in or getting ready to leave. Finally, he saw Ross motioning to him several yards ahead.

"Where is she?"

"Over there." Ross nodded across the room where Abigail was sitting, her head bowed and her eyes closed. "Her train isn't due in for about twenty minutes."

Marcus sighed in relief. She was still here. "Thank you, Ross."

He prayed with each step he took. *Dear Lord, please let her hear me out. Please let her forgive me. I ask Your forgiveness, too. And I ask that if it be Your will, I can convince her to share her life with me.*

He took the seat beside her, and she didn't even look up. He braced himself for the possibility that she might run from him, and then he took a deep breath. "Excuse me, miss. I'd like to ask your forgiveness if you can find a way to give it to me."

Abigail opened her eyes and started to rise. Marcus put a hand to her shoulder. "Please hear me out, Abigail. Please. I love you so."

She did stand then, shaking her head. "No. How could you? You've just found out all the bad there is to know about me."

Marcus jumped to his feet, his hands on her arms, looking deep into her eyes. "None of that—"

"You know how selfish and manipulative I've been in the past," she continued. "You know how I tried to get my sister's husband to marry—"

"No, Abigail. Don't—"

"—me when he loved someone else," she continued as if she didn't hear him. "You found out how I was just like the rest of my friends, only wanting to have—"

Marcus couldn't stand hearing her talk about herself that way. He stopped her the only way he knew how. He pulled her into his arms and pressed his lips against hers, stopping her words and trying to show her that none of what he knew mattered. Finally, she responded, and he deepened the kiss. It was several moments before he raised his lips from hers, and then he looked into her eyes. "I love you, Abigail. With all my heart. *None* of what I found out matters. You aren't that woman, and you haven't been for months."

"But—"

His fingers stilled her lips. "No buts. I love the woman you are. I shouldn't have looked into your past. But when you got here, you were so sad. . . . My only excuse is that I wanted, needed to know why. But I had no right. I should have asked you, not taken it on myself to find out. I knew as soon as I got the report that you weren't the same woman you'd been when you left Eureka Springs. That was made even clearer when your old crowd came into town."

"You didn't just find all this out when you looked into Robert's past?"

Marcus steeled himself for her wrath. "No. I knew before they ever got here. And I watched as you changed, a little each day, into the woman I've fallen in love with. Please, Abigail. Don't go. Please forgive me and give me a chance to win your love."

๛

Abigail felt her heart would explode with joy. Marcus loved her. And he'd fallen in love with her, knowing about her past. She shook her head. It was too good to believe.

"Oh, please don't say no, Abigail," Marcus said. "Just think about it—"

Her hand came up to cup his jaw. "I don't need to think, Marcus. I love you, too. I thought that you couldn't love me because—"

Marcus claimed her lips once more, cutting off her words and convincing her of his love. When he raised his head, he looked into her eyes and said, "No more talk about your past. From now on, there is only the future. Please, Abigail, will you do me the honor of becoming my wife?"

"Oh, Marcus, yes. Oh yes, I will." She stood on tiptoe and sealed her promise with a kiss meant to leave him with no doubt that she meant every word.

epilogue

October 16, 1886

Abigail had no desire to go back to Eureka Springs for the wedding. As soon as possible, she wanted to be married in Hot Springs, in the church where she'd begun to change and where she'd fallen in love with Marcus. She'd waited much too long for Nate to fall in love with her. She didn't want to wait one moment longer than she had to before becoming Mrs. Marcus Wellington.

She wrote home and asked her mother and father to come and bring the dress Meagan had made for her. She didn't want to wait to have another made, and neither did Marcus. They just wanted to get married as soon as possible. She'd hired Bea to come work for her and Marcus as housekeeper in the home they were having built. It would be ready to move into when they returned from their wedding trip to Europe.

They were married on a crisp fall day, and Abigail was overjoyed to have her family there to share the day with her. Marcus's parents were trying to talk hers into coming back for Thanksgiving, and Abigail hoped they'd stay through Christmas, too.

But what made her heart sing and made the day even more perfect as she walked down the aisle toward her groom was that Natalie went before her, sprinkling flower petals along the way, while Nate and Meagan sat beside her parents.

To be given so much—forgiveness from those she'd hurt so badly and the love of a man who loved her as she was. Her heart overflowed with happiness as she and Marcus said their vows, and her hand trembled as he slid an emerald ring that had belonged to his grandmother on her finger. All her dreams were coming true.

As soon as the minister declared them husband and wife, Marcus claimed her lips in a kiss that sealed their promises to each other. Her heart felt as if it might burst with happiness as they turned and walked back down the aisle. When they arrived in the church foyer, her new husband pulled her into his arms and whispered, "I love you, Abigail Wellington," just before his lips claimed hers once more.

Abigail kissed her new husband back and thanked the Lord above for the blessings He'd rained down on her—especially for forgiving her, for changing her, and for giving her a love all her own.

A Letter To Our Readers

Dear Reader:

In order that we might better contribute to your reading enjoyment, we would appreciate your taking a few minutes to respond to the following questions. We welcome your comments and read each form and letter we receive. When completed, please return to the following:

Fiction Editor
Heartsong Presents
PO Box 719
Uhrichsville, Ohio 44683

1. Did you enjoy reading *A Love All Her Own* by Janet Lee Barton?
   ❑ Very much! I would like to see more books by this author!
   ❑ Moderately. I would have enjoyed it more if

   _____

   _____

   _____

2. Are you a member of **Heartsong Presents**? ❑ Yes ❑ No
   If no, where did you purchase this book? _____

   _____

3. How would you rate, on a scale from 1 (poor) to 5 (superior), the cover design? _____

4. On a scale from 1 (poor) to 10 (superior), please rate the following elements.

   ____ Heroine   ____ Plot
   ____ Hero   ____ Inspirational theme
   ____ Setting   ____ Secondary characters

5. These characters were special because? _____

_____

_____

6. How has this book inspired your life? _____

_____

_____

7. What settings would you like to see covered in future
   Heartsong Presents books? _____

_____

_____

8. What are some inspirational themes you would like to see
   treated in future books? _____

_____

_____

9. Would you be interested in reading other **Heartsong
   Presents** titles? ❏ Yes ❏ No

10. Please check your age range:
    ❏ Under 18   ❏ 18-24
    ❏ 25-34   ❏ 35-45
    ❏ 46-55   ❏ Over 55

Name _____

Occupation _____

Address _____

City, State, Zip_____

WILD PRAIRIE ROSES

3 stories in 1

In the decade following the Civil War, rumors of gold lost near Browning City, Iowa, lead couples on quests for treasure. Three authors join to tell a three-part story.

Historical, paperback, 352 pages, 5⁵⁄₁₆" x 8"

_____

Please send me ____ copies of *Wild Prairie Roses.* I am enclosing $7.97 for each. (Please add $4.00 to cover postage and handling per order. OH add 7% tax. If outside the U.S. please call 740-922-7280 for shipping charges.)

Name_____

Address _____

City, State, Zip _____

To place a credit card order, call 1-740-922-7280.
Send to: Heartsong Presents Readers' Service, PO Box 721, Uhrichsville, OH 44683

Heart♥ong

Any 12
Heartsong
Presents titles
for only
$27.00*

HISTORICAL ROMANCE IS CHEAPER BY THE DOZEN!

Buy any assortment of twelve *Heartsong Presents* titles and save 25% off of the already discounted price of $2.97 each!

*plus $4.00 shipping and handling per order and sales tax where applicable. If outside the U.S. please call 740-922-7280 for shipping charges.

HEARTSONG PRESENTS TITLES AVAILABLE NOW:

(If ordering from this page, please remember to include it with the order form.)